Enjoy all of these American Girl Mysteries:

THE SILENT STRANGER
A *Kaya* Mystery

PERIL AT KING'S CREEK
A *Felicity* Mystery

SECRETS IN THE HILLS
A *Josefina* Mystery

THE STOLEN SAPPHIRE
A *Samantha* Mystery

THE CURSE OF RAVENSCOURT
A *Samantha* Mystery

DANGER AT THE ZOO
A *Kit* Mystery

A SPY ON THE HOME FRONT
A *Molly* Mystery

— A *Samantha* MYSTERY —

THE STOLEN SAPPHIRE

by Sarah Masters Buckey

★ American Girl™

Questions or comments? Call 1-800-845-0005, visit our Web site
at **americangirl.com**, or write Customer Service, American Girl,
8400 Fairway Place, Middleton, WI 53562-0497.

Printed in China
06 07 08 09 10 11 LEO 12 11 10 9 8 7 6 5 4 3 2 1

PICTURE CREDITS
The following individuals and organizations have generously given
permission to reprint illustrations contained in "Looking Back" and on the back
panel of the paperback cover: pp. 172–173—shipping poster, © Christie's
Images/Corbis; girl on ship deck, © Hulton-Deutsch Collection/Corbis;
pp. 174–175—ship departing, Mary Evans Picture Library; pp. 176–177—ship
lounge, © Hulton-Deutsch Collection/Corbis; steerage passengers, Getty
Images; Cobh harbor, © Geray Sweeney/Corbis; pp. 178–179—tourists in
Egypt, © Leonard de Selva/Corbis; *National Geographic* magazine,
courtesy of the National Geographic Society; Arthur Evans, © Hulton-Deutsch
Collection/Corbis; Star of India, Smithsonian Institution/American Museum
of Natural History; back panel of paperback cover—ruby, Smithsonian
Institution/American Museum of Natural History, gift of Mr. and Mrs.
Edward J. Slattery; Hope Diamond, Smithsonian Institution/American
Museum of Natural History, gift of Harry Winston, 1958; Hooker Emerald,
Smithsonian Institution/American Museum of Natural History,
gift of Mrs. Janet Annenberg Hooker, 1977.

Illustrations by Jean-Paul Tibbles

Cataloging-in-Publication Data
available from the Library of Congress.

For Alexandra

TABLE OF CONTENTS

1

A STRANGE ENCOUNTER

As snowflakes whirled through the air, Samantha Parkington wiggled her fingers inside her mittens and stomped her feet to keep warm. She looked out hopefully at the slushy New York City street. Shoppers were hurrying past Bertram's Book Shop, their hats pulled low to keep out the snow. But Samantha didn't see Nellie, her adopted sister and very best friend.

"Samantha, you're still here!" exclaimed a familiar voice.

White-haired Mr. Bertram stepped out of the store with a package in his hand. "Your aunt requested these books, and they were just delivered. I think they may be for your trip." Mr. Bertram's eyes twinkled. "Would you like to take them home?"

"Oh, yes!" Samantha said. Mr. Bertram handed her a square package wrapped in brown paper. She ran her mittened hand along the outside and felt the outline of two books. *One for me, one for Nellie?* she guessed.

Mr. Bertram scanned the sky. "Would you like to wait inside for Nellie? It's awfully cold out here."

Samantha hesitated. She *was* getting cold. But she and Nellie met outside Bertram's Book Shop every day after school, and Nellie was hardly ever late. "Thank you, but Nellie should be here any moment."

Just then, Samantha saw Nellie's blue coat hurrying toward her through the swirling snow. "There she is! Good-bye, Mr. Bertram!"

"I'm sorry I'm late," Nellie apologized as the two girls met. She held up the arithmetic book that she was carrying. "Miss Frantzen gave me problems to do while we're away." Nellie sighed. "I hope I don't fall too far behind in school."

Samantha nodded. She and Nellie were

sailing the next day on a voyage to Europe with their grandparents, Grandmary and Admiral Beemis. Samantha could hardly wait for the trip, but she knew she would have a lot of schoolwork to do while they were away.

"We'll both study on board the ship," she assured Nellie. "Miss Grise says I have to write an essay in French describing our trip." Samantha made a face. "I can hardly write a sentence in French—how can she expect me to do a whole essay?"

"What about the French tutor who's coming with us?" Nellie reminded her. "Your grandmother said she'll teach us French. Maybe she'll help you with your essay, too."

"Maybe," Samantha agreed. "But I hope she's not as strict as Miss Grise. Every time I make a mistake, Miss Grise sucks in her cheeks like she's eaten a lemon and says 'Tsk-tsk!'" Samantha shuddered at the memory. "If the French tutor is *anything* like Miss Grise, we'll have to find ways to get away from her."

"Tsk-tsk!" teased Nellie, puckering her face, and both girls giggled as they made their way down the snowy sidewalk.

"I'm glad we're going to miss school for a few weeks," admitted Samantha. "It'll be so exciting to travel around England *and* France! The Admiral said we'll dock overnight in Queenstown, too, so we'll be able to see the coast of Ireland from the ship."

"It'll be wonderful," agreed Nellie, hugging her book to her chest. "My mam used to say that she wished she could take me home to visit Ireland. She said it's the most beautiful place in the whole world." Nellie stopped, and Samantha knew she was remembering her mother, who had died of influenza.

For a few minutes the girls walked on together in silence. Then Nellie continued, "I've always hoped I'd see Ireland someday. And now I will—even if it's only from the ship. And we'll actually visit London and Paris." Nellie sighed as they stopped at a corner. "It's hard to believe."

Samantha nodded. *So much has changed for Nellie and me,* she thought.

Samantha's parents had died when she was little, and she'd lived most of her life with her grandmother in the small town of Mount Bedford, New York. Two years ago, while she was playing in the backyard of Grandmary's fancy house, Samantha had met Nellie O'Malley, the daughter of poor Irish immigrants. Although Nellie had to work as a servant, the two nine-year-old girls had quickly become best friends.

Then Samantha's Uncle Gard and Aunt Cornelia had gotten married, and they had invited Samantha to live with them in New York City. Samantha loved New York, but she had missed her friend. One day she'd learned that Nellie's parents had died and that Nellie and her sisters, Bridget and Jenny, were living in a terrible orphanage. Aunt Cornelia and Uncle Gard had decided to adopt all three O'Malley girls. Now Samantha finally had the sisters she'd always wanted.

I'm so glad that we're all a family, Samantha thought happily as she and Nellie waited for a horse-drawn carriage to pass. The tall carriage sped by, its wheels spraying icy slush. As Samantha jumped back to avoid being splattered, she bumped into someone standing behind her.

"Excuse me," Samantha apologized. She glanced up and saw a tall, thin boy in a worn coat, an old tweed cap, and a knitted blue scarf that covered most of his face. The boy, who looked to be about seventeen or eighteen, didn't reply. He just pulled his cap down and walked off in the opposite direction.

Samantha quickly caught up with Nellie, who had started across the street. As the girls hurried toward home through the falling snow, they talked excitedly of their upcoming trip.

"Maybe if it gets really cold, we can go ice-skating on the waves!" Samantha joked. She found an ice-slicked puddle and slid across it. "Like this!"

"Oohh!" said Nellie, sliding too. "I wonder if it snows in the middle of the ocean!"

The two girls turned into a quiet street where the fresh snow lay white and clean on the sidewalk. They were halfway down the block when a boy suddenly stepped out from between two houses. He stood in the center of the sidewalk, just a few feet ahead of them. As Samantha glanced at him, she felt a shock of surprise. She was almost sure that she recognized his tweed cap and blue scarf. It was the same boy she'd run into a few blocks before.

How did he get here? she wondered. *He was walking in the other direction.* A sudden fear swept over her, chilling her even more than the wind-blown snow. *Is he following us?*

Samantha looked around for the policeman who patrolled this neighborhood. She didn't see him anywhere, and the snow seemed to have driven everyone else inside. She and Nellie were alone with this strange boy. Samantha reached for Nellie's arm, hoping to steer her quickly to the other side of the street.

Nellie, however, fixed her eyes on the boy as he pulled the scarf from his face. "Oh! It's you, Jamie!" she exclaimed. "I hardly recognized you."

Samantha wasn't sure whether Nellie sounded relieved or worried.

Hands in his pockets, the boy walked toward them. "Aye, it's me," he told Nellie. "But it's you who looks different, Nellie O'Malley."

Nellie shrugged, but said nothing.

"Is it true you're goin' across the sea? Back to where we came from?" he asked, drawing so close that he now towered over Nellie.

Nellie nodded.

"I thought so," the boy said with satisfaction. "I saw you and your friend when you was shoppin' a few days ago, and I heard the lady with you talkin' about it. I said to myself, that's Nellie O'Malley, sure as life, and it looks like she's done all right for herself." The boy glanced at the neighboring houses. "When they sent me to deliver your package, I saw

you'd done more than all right. You live in
that fine house right on the park, don't you?"

"Jamie—" Nellie protested.

Scowling, the boy interrupted her. "I ain't
askin' for money. I only want to talk to you."
He looked pointedly at Samantha. "Alone."

Samantha remembered all of Aunt Cornelia's
warnings about strangers. "We should go
home," she whispered to Nellie.

"It's all right," Nellie whispered back. "I
know him." Then Nellie told the boy, "I can't
leave my friend."

The boy pointed at Samantha. "You stay
there," he told her. Then he looked at Nellie.
"And you come over here." He jerked his head,
and Nellie followed him a few feet into the
narrow side yard between the houses.

The falling snow stung Samantha's cheeks
as she stood alone on the sidewalk. Nellie's
back was to her, but Samantha could see that
the boy had a hard, determined expression on
his face. She watched as he reached into his
coat and pulled out a small package.

What does he want? Samantha wondered as she saw Nellie shake her head.

Feeling increasingly uneasy, Samantha stomped her boots on the frozen sidewalk and tried to warm her icy feet. The wind was beginning to blow harder, and as she turned her face from the snow, she was relieved to see the neighborhood policeman. He was coming toward them, walking quickly down the other side of the street. He paused when he saw Samantha, Nellie, and the boy in the threadbare coat.

The policeman hesitated for a moment as he peered through the driving snow. Then he called out, "Hey! You, boy!"

When the boy saw the patrolman heading in his direction, he said something to Nellie. Then he ran away through the side yard, back behind the houses.

"Stop!" the policeman shouted, racing after him.

The policeman disappeared behind the houses. But in a few minutes, he returned to

Samantha and Nellie. His round face was red and he was breathing hard. "Was that boy bothering you young ladies?" he demanded.

Samantha looked at Nellie questioningly. "No," Nellie answered. "He just asked for some help."

"Help? Is that what he calls it?" the policeman asked. "Well, don't trust him. Boys like him would rather beg and steal than do an honest day's work." He looked at the girls closely. "I've seen you young ladies often enough. You live nearby, don't you?"

"On the next block," said Samantha.

"Well, you'd better get home now. I'll make sure that young fellow doesn't bother you again." The policeman waited at the corner, pacing back and forth and watching as the girls hurried down the street.

As soon as they were far enough away, Samantha asked Nellie, "Who was that boy?"

"His name's Jamie O'Connor," Nellie said in a low tone.

"Is he a friend?"

Nellie kicked a piece of ice on the sidewalk before she answered. "His father helped my dad when we first moved here, and our families were friends. It's been a long time since I've seen Jamie, though."

She paused, and Samantha thought she was going to say something more. But then both girls heard a sharp voice calling, "Samantha! Nellie!"

Samantha saw a square of light glowing from their tall brownstone home a few houses away. Gertrude, their housekeeper, was standing in the doorway, looking out into the snowy dusk as she called for them.

"We're coming!" Samantha called back.

As the girls climbed the six marble steps that led from the sidewalk to their front door, Gertrude waited impatiently. "I can't believe you two would come home late from school today of all days!" she scolded as she helped them take off their coats and scarves in the foyer. "Where have you been?"

Nellie looked down at the floor, and

Samantha guessed that she didn't want to mention meeting Jamie. "Mr. Bertram gave me these," Samantha said, handing the package of books to Gertrude. "Aunt Cornelia ordered them."

"Oh yes, your aunt was hoping they'd arrive," said Gertrude, temporarily distracted. Then she continued briskly, "Now you girls had better get upstairs and check your trunks before I close them up. And then..."

With Gertrude's voice still chiding them, Samantha and Nellie hurried upstairs. In the center of their room, Samantha was thrilled to see two shiny black trunks, both filled with neatly packed clothes that smelled of washing soda and starch.

For a moment, she forgot her worries about Nellie and the strange boy. *Tomorrow,* she thought excitedly, *we'll be at sea!*

2
All Aboard

At three o'clock the next day, Samantha and Nellie were standing on the main deck of the R.M.S. *Queen Caroline.* As the wind whipped at their woolen coats, both girls looked out over the ship's railing and waved their white handkerchiefs.

"Good-bye!" they called toward the dock, where they could see Uncle Gard, Aunt Cornelia, Bridget, and Jenny waving to them.

Nellie was smiling bravely, but Samantha could see tears sliding down her cheeks. "Bridget and Jenny will be fine while we're gone," Samantha reassured her. "Aunt Cornelia's going to take them to the Wild West show, and Uncle Gard's going to take them skating in Central Park. And Bridget can hardly wait to start her violin lessons."

"I know," Nellie nodded, wiping her eyes with her handkerchief. She looked down at the ship's railing. "It's just that . . . well, ever since Mam and Dad died, Bridget and Jenny and I have always been together. I'll miss them."

I will, too, Samantha thought. As she reached for Nellie's hand, she heard Grandmary say gently, "Would you like another handkerchief, Nellie? It can be hard to say good-bye to one's family."

Samantha looked over and saw that Grandmary and Admiral Beemis were now standing beside Nellie at the ship's railing. The dignified, white-haired couple had married more than a year ago, and since then they had spent much of their time traveling together. Last spring, the Admiral and Grandmary had taken Samantha to London with them. This year, they had invited both Samantha and Nellie to accompany them on their trip to England and France.

Nellie had felt honored by the invitation, but she was not yet completely comfortable with her adopted grandparents. Once she had told Samantha, "Your grandmother is very nice, but she's just the way I'd always imagined a queen would be. And I don't know the Admiral very well, so it's hard to think of him as my grandfather!"

Now Nellie curtsied before she accepted the lace-trimmed handkerchief from Grandmary. "Thank you, ma'am," she said formally. "And I would like to thank you and Admiral Beemis for inviting me on this trip."

"Come, come, Nellie," the Admiral said heartily. "You are part of our family now and we're glad you could join us. It should be a jolly trip. I, for one, am truly looking forward to visiting Paris again."

He turned to the girls' new French tutor, Mademoiselle Nicole Étienne, who was standing just a few feet behind them. "And Mademoiselle, I'm sure you're looking forward to seeing your home again, aren't you?"

ALL ABOARD

"Oui, Monsieur," Mademoiselle Étienne told the Admiral. She was a small, slender young woman with large brown eyes and a hint of freckles sprinkled across her nose. "When I first came to this country as a tutor for the Larchmonts' children, I never imagined that I would stay here for two years. I am very happy to return home."

While Mademoiselle Étienne spoke, her eyes were anxiously scanning the dock as if she was searching for something or someone. *She doesn't look happy,* Samantha thought. *She looks worried.*

The Admiral, however, took a deep breath of the salty cold air and sighed contentedly. "Ah, it's good to be at sea again!" he announced. "And the *Queen Caroline* is as fine a ship as ever drew water. She may not have all the frills that modern ships do, but she's as solid and seaworthy as the best of them." He gestured at the towering masts above them, and Samantha saw the white sails tightly furled against the wood. "Look at those masts!

They're still as strong as the day they were built."

"It's a lovely ship," Grandmary agreed. "And so few passengers this time of year! We shall have a nice, quiet voyage, I'm sure."

Samantha listened to the masts creaking in the wind, and she felt a thrill. She knew that the ship's steam engines provided the main power for the voyage, but the tall masts gave the *Queen Caroline* an air of adventure. *If there's a storm and we lose all the engines, we could sail across the Atlantic,* she thought. *Wouldn't it be exciting to write home about that!*

As the crew lifted the ship's gangplanks, a steward in a white jacket walked by, ringing a shiny bell. "Tea is being served in the first-class saloon!" he announced. "Starboard, promenade deck."

Samantha saw that Nellie looked puzzled by the announcement. "A saloon is like a lounge," she whispered to Nellie. "'Starboard' means right, and left is 'port.'" Nellie nodded and then returned to waving her handkerchief.

"A cup of tea *would* be nice," said Grandmary. "Shall we all go upstairs? We can wave good-bye from the saloon's windows."

Samantha saw the flash of disappointment on Nellie's face. "Could Nellie and I please stay out here?" Samantha asked. "Just until we can't see the dock anymore?"

Mademoiselle Étienne offered to stay with the girls, and Grandmary agreed. "But don't get too chilled," she cautioned them. "It wouldn't do for you to catch pneumonia!"

The Admiral and Grandmary walked away arm in arm while Mademoiselle Étienne stood between Samantha and Nellie at the railing. There was a loud blast of the ship's horn, and then the *Queen Caroline* began to slowly steam out of the harbor.

"Good-bye!" Samantha called out again and again to her family on the shore, her voice becoming slightly hoarse.

"Au revoir!" Mademoiselle Étienne corrected her.

For a moment, Samantha's heart fell. *It's*

going to be like having Miss Grise with me for the whole trip! she thought.

Then she saw that the French tutor was smiling. Mademoiselle Étienne had a friendly smile, with dimples in her cheeks. Samantha smiled back at her. *"Au revoir!"* she called as the figures on the dock became smaller and smaller.

"Thank heavens we're finally leaving!" a girl's voice exclaimed. Samantha turned and saw that a girl with an upturned nose and blond ringlets had taken a place beside her at the railing. The girl examined Samantha critically. "Only first-class passengers are allowed in this area," she said, frowning. "You *are* in first class, aren't you?"

The girl looked at her so accusingly that Samantha suddenly wasn't quite sure. She knew that first-class tickets were the most expensive. People with more moderate incomes traveled second class, while poor people traveled in steerage. Samantha decided that the Admiral and Grandmary wouldn't have bought second-class or steerage tickets, so she answered, "Yes, we're in first class."

"Really?" the girl continued. She sounded skeptical. "My mother said there aren't many other first-class passengers on this voyage— besides the famous archaeologist, of course."

"Famous archaeologist?" echoed Samantha.

"Haven't you heard?" asked the girl, arching her pale eyebrows. "Professor Fitzwilliam Wharton is aboard this ship. He's taking the famous Blue Star sapphire to London."

Mademoiselle Étienne suddenly leaned in to join the conversation. "Excuse me," she asked in her accented English, speaking loudly to be heard above the wind. "Did you say that the Blue Star sapphire—it is on this ship?"

"Yes, and I saw Professor Wharton come aboard, too," the girl reported. "He had a strange-looking dog with him in a cage, and men from the newspapers were following him, asking him about the Blue Star." The girl smiled knowingly. "Everyone says that the Blue Star is unlucky, but it's supposed to be one of the most beautiful jewels in the whole world, and I want to see it."

"But of course!" agreed Mademoiselle Étienne.

Samantha leaned over to call to Nellie. "Did you hear?" she asked above the wind. "The Blue Star sapphire is aboard this ship!"

"Uncle Gard was reading about that in the papers," Nellie replied as she continued to wave toward the shrinking figures on the shore. "Wasn't it taken from India?"

"It once belonged to a king, but it was stolen from Ceylon hundreds of years ago," the blond girl corrected Nellie loudly. Then she turned her attention back to Samantha. "Everyone thought the Blue Star was gone forever," she continued. "But Professor Wharton spent years searching for it. Finally, he found it buried in a graveyard in Central America. Can you imagine—who would hide a king's sapphire in a graveyard?"

Samantha shivered at the thought of hiding *anything* in a graveyard. "No, I can't imagine," she told the girl truthfully.

The girl studied her for a moment. She seemed to decide that Samantha passed inspection. "I'm Charlotta Billingsley," she announced. "I'm twelve. How old are you?"

"Eleven."

"I don't know your name," said Charlotta, as if this were somehow Samantha's fault.

Samantha quickly introduced herself, along with Mademoiselle Étienne and Nellie.

"I didn't bring my nanny. My parents say I'm too old for one, anyway," said Charlotta, casting a critical eye on Mademoiselle Étienne.

Mademoiselle Étienne bit her lip, and then turned to Samantha and Nellie. "We should go to our cabin and unpack, *n'est-ce pas?*" she suggested.

Samantha and Nellie followed their tutor across the main deck, and then through a door that led to a stairway. The ship was rising and falling in the choppy waves, so Samantha stayed close to the brass banister as she walked carefully down the steep wooden stairs.

When she heard heavy footsteps behind her, she tried to go a little faster. Then suddenly, something warm and furry fell onto her shoulders. A long tail fluttered in front of her face, tickling her nose.

"Aagghh!" she cried out, stumbling in surprise.

3
AN UNLUCKY STAR

Samantha reached out for the brass banister and caught herself from falling down the stairs. She heard a man's voice behind her. "Stop that, Plato!" he ordered. "Come here!"

There was a screech of protest. Then Samantha felt tiny hands grasping her hair. Suddenly, she was face-to-face with a little brown monkey, its round eyes looking appealingly into hers.

The man hurried up beside her. "Dreadfully sorry!" he said as he snatched the monkey from Samantha. Samantha turned and saw a tall, athletic-looking young man with wavy dark hair and wire-rimmed glasses. "Plato's a naughty little fellow," he said apologetically. "He's always getting into mischief."

The monkey held on to the lapels of the man's coat like a baby clutching its mother. Chattering excitedly, the little animal turned to watch Samantha, his wide eyes examining her intently.

"Are you hurt?" asked Mademoiselle, who was waiting at the bottom of the stairs with Nellie. They had both turned around when Samantha called out, and Mademoiselle now sounded concerned.

"I'm fine," Samantha assured Mademoiselle. "I was just surprised."

Samantha held out her hand to the monkey, and he gently grasped it as if they were shaking hands. "Is your monkey's name Plato?" she asked the young man.

"Yes," he said as they continued down the stairs. "But he's not really mine. My uncle, Professor Wharton, found him a few weeks ago in a marketplace in Central America. The other monkeys were picking on this little one, so my uncle bought him to rescue him from the bullies. Now Plato goes everywhere with us.

My uncle even had a special cage made for him, but Plato prefers to be out exploring."

Samantha realized the "odd-looking dog" that Charlotta had seen with Professor Wharton had probably been this long-tailed monkey. She smiled to herself to think that perhaps Charlotta didn't know as much as she pretended to.

They had reached the foot of the stairs, and the young man bowed politely to Mademoiselle Étienne and Nellie. "I'm sorry that Plato disturbed you, ladies."

"He's sweet," said Nellie, reaching out to touch the monkey's soft fur. "I knew an organ grinder's monkey that could do clever tricks. Does Plato do tricks, too?"

"Not yet," said the young man as he opened a door labeled *First Class Cabins* and ushered Samantha, Nellie, and Mademoiselle Étienne through it. "Though my uncle is sure he's very intelligent."

Plato nodded and chattered as if he agreed with this last statement. They had entered a corridor with white walls and polished wood floors. Both sides of the corridor were lined with numbered doors, and Samantha guessed that these were the cabins.

"Personally," the young man continued, "I think the little creature is more mischievous than clever. My uncle doesn't agree, though, and he's the boss. I'm just traveling as his assistant. Oh, excuse me, I haven't introduced myself—my name's Harrison Wharton III, but please call me Harry."

Mademoiselle Étienne introduced the girls and herself as they walked down the corridor. "You're their French tutor?" Harry exclaimed to her. "Why, I assumed you were the girls' older sister. Are you from Paris? I spent two wonderful years there . . ."

Harry and Mademoiselle Étienne began to speak rapidly in French. Samantha caught a few words here and there— Mademoiselle Étienne mentioned that she had taught the Larchmont children; Harry talked about living in Paris—but most of what they said was incomprehensible to her.

Plato, meanwhile, peeked over Harry's shoulder, and Samantha and Nellie waved to him. He eagerly waved his tiny hand back at them and clucked his tongue as if he wanted to join the conversation, too.

Mademoiselle stopped in front of Cabin 7. "Good day, *Monsieur*," she said, and then she added with a smile, "Good day, Plato."

Harry tipped his hat. "Plato and I shall hope to see you ladies later."

As Harry continued down the corridor, Mademoiselle opened the door to their cabin. Inside, Grandmary's maid, Doris, straightened her apron as she met them. She was a tall, thin, elderly woman who was quite hard of hearing. "I just finished unpacking your trunks," she announced loudly to Samantha and Nellie. "And the Admiral says to tell you that he'll be by at seven to take you to dinner."

"Thank you!" Samantha answered at the top of her voice. Doris smiled and nodded as she left the room.

Samantha looked around. "Jiminy!" she exclaimed. "This is how I always thought a ship's cabin *should* look."

On Samantha's first voyage with her grandparents, they had sailed on a large, modern ship, the S.S. *Londonia*. The trip had been wonderful, but Samantha had felt almost as if she were steaming across the ocean in an elegant hotel.

The *Queen Caroline*, however, was a much smaller, older ship. It was clean and neat, but, as the Admiral had said, there were no modern frills. Every inch of space in their cabin was carefully used. Bookshelves and a wooden table were built into the walls. Straight-backed chairs flanked the table, and just above it, a porthole let in light and offered a view of the choppy waves outside.

"It's very nice," agreed Nellie, a little uncertainly. "But where do we sleep?"

"Voilà!" said Mademoiselle Étienne, smiling. She gestured toward a door on the left that blended into the wood paneling. Then she

motioned toward a door on the opposite side of the room. "And my bed is there."

Samantha and Nellie opened the door to their bedroom. It was so small that Samantha felt as if she'd stepped inside a giant cupboard, but the neatly arranged space had its own porthole, a closet, built-in drawers, and a pair of berths—one upper and one lower.

"I've always wanted a bed like this," Samantha said as she climbed to the upper berth. She ran her hands over the soft, red woolen blankets. They smelled like ocean air. "Haven't you?"

"I've slept in bunk beds before," Nellie admitted as she climbed up the ladder, too. "But they weren't nearly as nice as this!"

First the girls sat on the top berth, leaning over so that they wouldn't hit their heads on the low ceiling. Next they looked into the drawers where Doris had put away their things. Samantha found Clara, her Nutcracker doll, and Nellie took out her doll, Lydia. Then both girls brought out the books

Aunt Cornelia had given them as *bon voyage* presents.

"Oh, it's *Treasure Island*!" Samantha exclaimed as she unwrapped her book. "It'll be easy to imagine that I'm on the ship with pirates!"

"I got *Alice's Adventures in Wonderland*!" Nellie reported. "Aunt Cornelia knew I wanted to read it."

Holding tight to *Treasure Island*, Samantha looked longingly at their bunk beds. She wanted to curl up on the top berth and read until it was time to get ready for dinner—but she was sure Nellie would want that berth, too. Samantha hesitated. Then she had an idea. "You can have the top berth for the first half of the trip," she offered. "Would you mind if I had it for the second half?"

"I wouldn't mind at all," Nellie said as she sank down on the lower berth. "But I'd rather take this bed first."

Samantha noticed that Nellie looked pale. "What's wrong?"

"I think . . ." Nellie glanced out the window at the churning seas, then groaned and buried her face in the pillow. "I think it's the ocean!"

At exactly seven o'clock, the Admiral knocked on the cabin door to escort the ladies to the dining room. Mademoiselle Étienne opened the door. "Ah, Samantha," she said, smiling, "it is your *grand-père*."

"*Grand-père!*" the Admiral exclaimed. He looked very distinguished in his black evening suit and topcoat. "Why, I like the sound of that even better than 'the Admiral.'"

"*Bonsoir, Grand-père!*" Samantha said with a polite curtsy. She was wearing a crimson satin dress, white lace gloves, and her new black high-button boots, all polished and shiny. But she was the only one in the cabin ready to go out for dinner.

"Please excuse us, sir, but Nellie and I both have the *mal de mer*," Mademoiselle Étienne explained to the Admiral. "I think it would be best if we did not go to dinner tonight."

"Well, Samantha, your grandmother is a bit

seasick, too, so it will be just the two of us," the Admiral said. He bowed and held out his arm. "Shall we go?"

Samantha felt elegant as she walked up to the main deck with her grandfather, her gloved hand resting lightly on his arm. They passed by the first-class dining room, which looked dark and deserted. The Admiral said that, since there were only about a dozen first-class passengers on this voyage, they all would be eating in the Captain's own dining room.

Farther down the hall, the Admiral opened a door labeled *Private Dining Room.* He ushered Samantha into a warm room that smelled temptingly of roasted turkey. A large round table filled most of the room. Silverware and crystal glasses gleamed on the table, which was covered with a delicate lace tablecloth laid over a starched linen cloth. The only illumination in the room came from the center of the table, where several candles burned in the branches of a silver candelabra.

Light from the candles danced on the faces gathered around the table. A distinguished-looking man with steel-gray hair and a short beard stood up as Samantha and her grandfather entered the room. "Admiral Beemis!" he said, smiling. "It's good to see you again after all these years, sir. I'm honored to have you and your family aboard my ship."

"Jolly good to sail with you, Captain Newman," declared the Admiral as the two men shook hands. The Captain introduced the Admiral and Samantha to Mr. and Mrs. Billingsley and Charlotta, and Samantha took a seat between her grandfather and Charlotta. Then she heard a clamor near the door.

Samantha looked up and saw Harry with a much older man, who she thought must be his uncle. Both men wore wire-rimmed glasses and formal dinner jackets with white bow ties, but unlike Harry, who was tall and handsome, Professor Wharton was short and round. He had pink cheeks and was bald, except for a fringe of white hair above his ears.

A blond man in a tweed jacket was following close behind Harry and his uncle. "Excuse me, Professor Wharton, I'm Jack Jackson, reporter for the *New York Daily Journal*," he announced in a rapid-fire voice. "I booked a ticket on this ship just so I could do a special story about the Blue Star sapphire. I have a couple of questions for you—"

"Excuse me, Mr. Jackson, my uncle is about to have dinner," Harry said stiffly, towering over the reporter.

The reporter pulled out his pencil and notepad eagerly. He was small and wiry, and he reminded Samantha of an energetic terrier. "This will take just a few minutes," he assured Harry. Then he turned back to Professor Wharton. "Sir, what about the Blue Star's history of bringing bad luck to whoever carries it? Will its bad luck follow it across the ocean?"

Captain Newman nodded to a steward, who stepped forward and grasped the reporter's arm. "This dining room is reserved for first-class passengers only, sir."

"I'll talk with you later, Professor," the reporter called over his shoulder as the steward escorted him out of the dining room.

Professor Wharton and Harry took seats across the table from Samantha. She wondered where Plato was, and Harry seemed to read her mind. "Plato felt a bit under the weather," he told her. "We had to leave him in the cabin."

"Yes, he wasn't himself at all, poor little fellow," agreed the Professor, pushing his glasses up on his nose. "I wouldn't have guessed that a monkey would become seasick. Fascinating how human they are, isn't it?"

Two stewards in white jackets began serving the dinner's first course, a steaming clam chowder. Samantha had never tried clam chowder before and she took her first sip cautiously. "This is delicious," she said.

"It's not bad," Charlotta agreed. "Where's your sister Ellie?"

"Nellie," Samantha corrected her. "She's not feeling well."

"Many people don't do well on ships, especially at first," said Charlotta authoritatively. She took another spoonful of chowder. "How old is Nellie?"

"Eleven, like me."

Charlotta studied her. "You don't *look* like twins," she said.

"We're adopted sisters."

"Adopted?" Charlotta echoed. She continued to ask questions until Samantha had to explain how Nellie, Bridget, and Jenny had been adopted by Uncle Gard and Aunt Cornelia.

"Your aunt and uncle adopted *servant* girls?" Charlotta looked shocked.

"They're not servants now—we're all a family," Samantha said, feeling increasingly uncomfortable with the conversation. She was glad when the stewards brought in the turkey, stuffing, and cranberry sauce. As she bent over her plate, she heard Mrs. Billingsley ask the Professor, "Is it true the sapphire brings bad luck wherever it goes? How thrilling!"

"No, Madam," the Professor said, shaking his head so hard that his glasses shifted. "That's all entirely foolish superstition."

Mrs. Billingsley, a plump woman who was wearing an impressive diamond necklace, looked a bit disappointed until Harry spoke up. "Surely, Uncle, you will admit that the Blue Star sapphire has had a long and, ah, *interesting* history."

The Professor put down his knife and fork. "Well, yes," he confessed, pushing his glasses back up on his nose. "It's quite shocking how many people have committed crimes to obtain the Blue Star. A merchant is said to have killed his brother over it. And a princess paid a fortune for the Blue Star and then disappeared quite mysteriously. And, of course, the whole reason the Blue Star ended up in a graveyard halfway around the world was because—"

The Professor suddenly noticed that all other conversation at the table had stopped.

Everyone was listening intently to him. His cheeks turned even pinker. "But this is hardly a suitable topic for dinner, especially with children present," he apologized. "The jewel's real importance is historical. It was prized by kings and it's a symbol of a great culture, just like the pyramids of the Egyptian pharaohs or the crown jewels of England's kings."

I wish I could see it, Samantha thought longingly.

Mrs. Billingsley voiced her thoughts. "Professor, we simply *must* see this magnificent stone," she pleaded. "Where do you keep it—in a vault somewhere?"

The Professor patted the breast pocket of his dinner jacket. "Madam, I carry the Blue Star with me at all times." Then he picked up his knife and fork again. "Now, however, is not the time for a display—we must give all our attention to this fine dinner."

Captain Newman steered the conversation to other topics. But after dinner was over and the stewards had removed the last dishes from the table, Mrs. Billingsley brought up the jewel again. "Professor," she implored, fingering the diamond pendant on her necklace, "do you think you might now be able to give us all the tiniest peek at the Blue Star? It would be such an honor to see it."

"Well..." the Professor hesitated.

"What's the harm in it?" Mr. Billingsley urged. He was a stout man with small, close-set eyes. He looked around the circle of faces at the table and smiled broadly. "Surely you can trust all of us here."

"Very well," the Professor agreed. He didn't seem too reluctant, and Samantha guessed that he enjoyed showing others his prized possession. "Harry, please lock the door," the Professor directed. "I don't want anyone to come in."

As Harry followed his uncle's instructions, Professor Wharton stood up and removed a small, dark green box from his breast pocket. Holding the box cupped in one hand, he pulled out his key ring and unlocked the box with a tiny key. Samantha bent forward in her chair as Professor Wharton carefully placed the closed box in the center of the table, right beneath the flickering lights of the candelabra.

The Professor stepped back for a moment. "Ladies and gentlemen," he announced dramatically. He paused, reached forward, and lifted the lid of the box. "The Blue Star."

There was a gasp around the table, as everyone leaned forward to see the shimmering blue sapphire. The radiant jewel was almost as big as a polished chestnut, and it caught the candlelight and glowed against its bed of dark velvet.

"Look closely, and you can see the star within it," the Professor advised.

Leaning even farther toward the gleaming jewel, Samantha saw a distinct pattern within the stone, like a tiny starfish caught in blue ice.

For a few moments, there was a tense silence in the room. Then Mrs. Billingsley asked in a choked voice, "How—how much would it cost?" She was staring at the stone as if transfixed.

"It's not for sale," Professor Wharton said curtly.

"I collect fine jewels myself, and I know that anything can be bought," Mr. Billingsley protested. "It's just a question of price. What's your price, sir?"

Samantha was shocked by Mr. Billingsley's rudeness, but Harry answered him politely. "That may usually be the case, sir. But my uncle is determined that the Blue Star be given to a museum."

"Indeed I am," said Professor Wharton. He retrieved the box, and closed and locked it. "A treasure like this should be shared with the whole world," he declared as he slipped the box back into his innermost pocket. "And I intend to personally hand the Blue Star to museum officials in London."

"Since the stone is so valuable, why don't we put it into the ship's safe?" suggested Captain Newman.

Harry coughed significantly. "According to legend, anyone who carries the Blue Star will suffer bad luck," he explained. "Of course, it's a foolish superstition, but my uncle and I nonetheless feel it's our responsibility to carry the stone ourselves."

The Captain's thick brows came together. "Very well," he said after a moment's thought. "I respect your decision. But I cannot guarantee the Blue Star's safety."

As she watched the Professor and Harry leave the dining room, Samantha tried to convince herself that the Blue Star was just a jewel. *It can't bring bad luck to anyone,* she told herself. But as she heard cold winds howl outside, she felt a shiver of fear.

4
STORMY WEATHER

The next morning dawned gray and windy, and the *Queen Caroline* continued to heave up and down through restless waves. Because of the bad weather, breakfast was served in the cabins. A friendly steward, who introduced himself as Oliver, brought plates of eggs, ham, kippered herring, toast, and fresh doughnuts, along with milk, coffee, and tea.

The sea air made Samantha hungry. She was enthusiastically enjoying her breakfast until she looked around and realized that she was the only one eating. Mademoiselle Étienne was just sipping weak tea, and Nellie was staring at a piece of toast as if she didn't dare to bring it to her mouth. "I'm sorry," said Samantha, putting down her half-eaten doughnut.

"No, *ma chérie,* please do not be sorry," Mademoiselle Étienne said, smiling. "You should eat. It will keep you strong. We will eat soon, too. In the meantime, tell us about last night."

"Yes," Nellie urged. "What does the sapphire look like?"

Encouraged by their interest, Samantha told them all about the evening. When she described the sapphire, Mademoiselle Étienne asked doubtfully, "How big do you say it is?"

"Almost this size," said Samantha, forming a circle with her thumb and forefinger.

"Incredible!" Mademoiselle gasped.

"It sparkled as if it had fire inside it," Samantha told them. "And the Professor said it's more than just a jewel. It once belonged to kings, and it's important historically, like the Egyptian pyramids or the crown jewels of England."

"I think a stone like that would be worth almost anything," Mademoiselle Étienne said eagerly. For a moment she seemed lost in thought. Then she drew herself up. "We should start our lessons, yes?"

Just then, the Admiral knocked on the door. He suggested that they go up to the promenade deck and sit in the first-class saloon. "The fresh air will do you good," he counseled. "And the girls can learn French every bit as well up there as they can in the cabin."

"Oui, Monsieur," Mademoiselle Étienne agreed, and they packed up their books. They followed the Admiral up two flights of stairs to the promenade deck. At the top of the stairs, he opened a door into a narrow, covered passageway. There was a wall on the left, but on the right there was only a waist-high railing. Samantha shuddered slightly as she looked several stories down toward the white-crested waves. *I'd hate to fall into that cold water,* she thought.

At the end of the passageway, they opened another door. "Watch out," the Admiral cautioned as they stepped over the door's foot-high threshold. "These thresholds are high so that water won't wash in during a storm." They passed through a small foyer, and then through another watertight door into the saloon. It was a cheerful room with wide windows that gave a clear view of the sea. Near the windows were tables and chairs for writing letters or playing cards and overstuffed sofas for reading or relaxing.

Mademoiselle Étienne led Samantha and Nellie to a small table, and they began reviewing French verbs. Every time the girls gave a correct answer, Mademoiselle Étienne would put a penny in a small jar. "When the jar is full, we will stop the lesson for this morning, yes?"

This isn't so bad, Samantha thought after another penny clinked into the jar. *It's more like a game than work.*

Nellie was in the middle of reciting the forms of "to run" when Charlotta wandered over to their table. She stood silently by Samantha's chair for a moment, listening to Nellie's answer. When Nellie had finished,

Charlotta smiled. "That's quite good, Nellie! Of course, your accent needs work, but I think it's lovely that you are trying to improve yourself. You must be so grateful that you've been adopted into better society!"

Nellie's cheeks went bright red. She flashed a glance at Samantha as if to ask, *What have you told this girl about me?*

Before Samantha could say anything, though, Charlotta continued. "It's nice that you're studying your French, too, Samantha. I'd love to study with you, but of course, I've been speaking it since I was old enough to say *maman*!"

Charlotta trilled a little laugh and then began a rapid conversation in French with Mademoiselle Étienne. After a few minutes, Charlotta departed with a cheerful *"Au revoir!"* Mademoiselle looked annoyed, and Samantha wondered if Charlotta had insulted her, too.

"Let us get back to our lesson," said Mademoiselle. "The penny jar is almost full."

In half an hour, they were finished. Nellie, who had been looking increasingly pale during the lesson, told Samantha that she was going back to their cabin to lie down.

Samantha decided to visit Grandmary in Cabin 8. When she knocked on the cabin door, Doris opened it for her. Grandmary was sitting in a chair, doing needlepoint. She was immaculately dressed, as always, but she looked tired.

"How are you feeling?" Samantha asked, settling into a chair beside her and taking in the lavender scent Grandmary always wore.

"A bit under the weather," Grandmary admitted with a smile. "But I'll find my sea legs soon. How are you and Nellie?"

Samantha explained that Nellie and Mademoiselle Étienne had been "under the weather," too. "Nellie was feeling better," Samantha added, "but she just went to our cabin to lie down."

"There is another girl about your age on the ship," Grandmary told Samantha. "I spoke with her mother, Mrs. Billingsley, yesterday afternoon. Mrs. Billingsley asked me all about Mademoiselle Étienne. She said that she wished she'd arranged French lessons for her daughter, Charlotta."

So much for Charlotta's perfect French, Samantha thought.

"Perhaps you and Charlotta could spend time together while Nellie rests," Grandmary suggested. "You might even practice your French together."

"Perhaps," Samantha said vaguely.

"You needn't spend all your time with Nellie," Grandmary urged. "It would be nice if you met other young ladies your age, too."

If only Grandmary knew Charlotta! Samantha thought. She sat in silence as Grandmary stitched. The small needlepoint canvas showed a ship at sea. "That looks pretty," Samantha commented at last.

"Thank you, dear," said Grandmary. "It's a bookmark. I'm making it for someone special as a memento of this trip." A smile creased the corners of Grandmary's bright blue eyes, and Samantha hoped the bookmark might be intended for her.

Samantha decided to ask something she had been wondering about. "Grandmary, why aren't we going to leave the ship when we stop in Queenstown? Could we visit there?"

Grandmary looked surprised. "Why, Samantha, Queenstown is not a place for travelers to visit. The ship is only making a short stop there to drop off and pick up mail. Some of the steerage passengers will be leaving the ship, of course, but they are Irish people who are returning to their homes."

"Nellie says that Ireland is very beautiful," Samantha ventured.

"Perhaps it is, dear," Grandmary replied as she concentrated on her needlework. "But it would be most unusual for travelers to go out of their way to visit there."

Samantha knew by the tone in her grandmother's voice that there was no point in discussing the question any further.

The *Queen Caroline* rode through rough seas all afternoon. Samantha and Nellie watched the waves smash against their porthole and heard icy rain beating down on the ship. By evening, the storm had become even worse.

"We're in for a bit of weather," the Admiral advised them. "Captain Newman expects it to last a couple of days—not unusual this time of year, but a bother all the same, I'm afraid. Meals will be brought to the cabins, and the upper promenade deck is closed for the time being."

"Then we can't go to the saloon?" Samantha asked.

"No, I'm afraid not," said the Admiral. "The outside decks can get quite slick in heavy rain. Passengers, especially children, have been known to fall overboard from slippery decks. And once they fall, they're often never seen again, especially in this kind of weather. Best to stay inside."

For the next two days, the *Queen Caroline* pitched and tossed through violent seas.

Samantha didn't mind the waves too much herself, but she felt sorry for Nellie, who spent most of her time in her berth.

Although Mademoiselle Étienne suffered from seasickness, too, she tried hard to keep up French lessons for Samantha. They played a game in which Mademoiselle would point to a common object, such as a button or a coffee cup. If Samantha knew the French word for the object, a penny would clink into the lesson jar. Samantha enjoyed the game because Mademoiselle was always encouraging and cheerful.

Only once did Mademoiselle become upset. She and Samantha were in the tutor's room, and Mademoiselle was pointing to her blankets, books, and other objects. Samantha noticed a framed portrait of an elderly gentleman on a shelf near the bed. She asked the tutor about it.

"That is my *grand-père*," Mademoiselle explained with a smile. "My parents died when I was small, and so my *grand-père* has been like a mother and a father to me." She lifted up the portrait and looked at it lovingly. "It will be good to see him again."

As Mademoiselle picked up the portrait, Samantha saw a small silver frame behind it. Inside the frame, a single dried rose was arranged behind the glass. Samantha knew that the word for *flower* was *fleur,* but she didn't know how to say *dried.* "What is this?" she asked, picking it up for a closer look.

Mademoiselle took the frame out of Samantha's hand and put it back on the shelf, hiding it behind her grandfather's portrait. "It is just a flower someone gave me once," she said abruptly. "Leave it there, please."

Samantha was puzzled by the tutor's reaction, but Mademoiselle soon regained her good humor. When the lesson was over, she suggested that Samantha might like some exercise. "It is too dangerous to walk on the promenade deck," the tutor warned. "But you may walk where you wish in the other first-class areas. And do not worry about

Nellie," she added kindly. "I will stay here with her."

Freed from her lessons, Samantha paid a visit to Grandmary, and they chatted together until Grandmary became tired. Then Samantha set off to explore the *Queen Caroline*. She walked through the first-class corridors and discovered that, since most of the cabins were empty, the whole area had an odd, deserted feeling. When she tried to visit the decks below, she met the steward, Oliver, coming up the stairs with a tray in his hands.

"You'd best not walk down there, Miss," he cautioned. "The next deck is second class, and below that is steerage. Not a proper place for a young lady, Miss."

"Oh," said Samantha, disappointed. On the *Londonia*, she had made friends with an immigrant girl who was traveling in the crowded, windowless rooms of the steerage section. Samantha wished she could see what it was like for steerage passengers aboard the *Queen Caroline*, but she knew she wasn't supposed to leave the first-class section. She followed Oliver back up the stairs.

I guess I'll read in the cabin, Samantha thought. *At least I'm feeling well.*

But the storm continued through the next day and night, and by the second night, even Samantha was queasy. To make matters worse, the ship's electrical generator failed in the midst of the stormy evening. Oliver brought a pair of oil lamps to their cabin, but the lamps gave off a foul-smelling smoke and had to be used sparingly. Lying in the darkness and feeling miserable, Samantha began to wonder if dawn would ever come.

On the morning of the third day, however, the storm began to clear. There still were no electric lights, but by afternoon a glimmer of sun was shining through the portholes. The Captain announced that dinner would once again be served in the private dining room.

Mademoiselle Étienne and Nellie decided that they felt well enough to attend the dinner.

Samantha was fastening the last button on her
blue velvet dress when the Admiral knocked
at the door. He explained that Grandmary
still felt too ill to go to dinner and sent her
apologies. "But I'm honored to escort three
such lovely ladies," he said gallantly as they
walked through the ship's halls, now dimly lit
by hanging oil lamps.

They arrived at the dining room a few
minutes early and found Harry already seated
at the table. *"Bonsoir!"* he said, politely
standing as they entered.

"Bonsoir," Mademoiselle answered with a
smile as they took their seats on the other side
of the table. Soon the Professor hurried in,
with Plato chattering on his shoulder.
Samantha had to suppress a giggle when she
saw the little monkey. He was wearing a tiny
white bow tie that matched the Professor's
formal tie.

"Didn't want the little fellow to miss all
the fun," the Professor explained, a little
sheepishly. "But I thought he should be

dressed for the occasion."

The reporter, Jack Jackson, followed the Professor into the dining room. "Excuse me, sir—" the steward objected, but just then Captain Newman entered.

"It's all right," Captain Newman told the steward. "Mr. Jackson has decided to buy a first-class ticket."

"I'm sure my editors would want me to dine with the famous Professor Wharton," Mr. Jackson told the other passengers. "They won't object to paying a little extra money for me to travel first class."

The reporter tried to sit down next to Harry, but Harry put his hand across the empty seat. "We're saving this seat for Plato."

"I suppose he paid first class too, eh?" said the reporter jovially. He slipped into a chair next to Nellie. "No matter. I'll sit next to this young lady."

The Billingsley family entered a moment later. Mrs. Billingsley, as the eldest lady present, sat in the place of honor by the

Captain's right. Mr. Billingsley took a seat next to his wife, and Charlotta sat down between her father and Samantha. On Samantha's other side was the Admiral; then, seated counter-clockwise around the table, came Mademoiselle Étienne, Nellie, Mr. Jackson, Plato, Harry, and finally, on the Captain's left, Professor Wharton.

Captain Newman looked around the full table. "Well, everyone is now here, so we can begin." While the passengers began their soup course, a steward gravely handed Plato his own small dish of parsley and orange slices.

During dinner, Samantha enjoyed watching Plato's antics. Whenever the little monkey could slip away from the Professor and Harry, he would roam the dining room. He climbed up one paneled wall and hung off a porthole window that had been left slightly ajar. Soon after Harry retrieved him from the porthole, Plato discovered the bellpull that summoned the steward. He scampered up the rope, dinging the bell loudly.

"I'm dreadfully sorry," the Professor apologized as the bell rang and a steward appeared. "I've had him only a month or so. He's not really trained yet."

Mrs. Billingsley gave a tight smile. Samantha wondered if she was annoyed by Plato but didn't want to offend the Professor by saying so.

After dinner, Mr. Thatcher, the ship's first mate, came into the dining room and asked for the Captain's opinion on a navigation question. Captain Newman invited the Admiral to accompany him to the bridge, and the two men excused themselves.

Once the table had been cleared and the stewards had left the room, Harry spoke up. "What shall we do for entertainment? Shall we play charades?"

Samantha thought charades would be great fun, but Mrs. Billingsley interjected. "I hoped you might show us the sapphire again, Professor," she said in a tone that suggested it was more of an order than a request. "Several people here did not have a chance to see it the other night."

There was an enthusiastic chorus of approval around the table. Professor Wharton held out his hands in a gesture of surrender. "As you wish," he agreed.

Harry locked the door and then quickly took his seat again, still firmly holding on to Plato. The Professor stood up and pulled the locked jewel box out of his pocket. Just as he had done the previous night, he unlocked the box and placed it, still closed, under the flickering light of the candelabra. Then he stepped back and announced, "Ladies and gentlemen, the Blue Star."

As the Professor reached over to open the box, Samantha suddenly felt the tablecloth jerk. She heard a crash as the candelabra fell. There was a smell of melting wax as the overturned candles sputtered and smoked. Then the room went black.

5

THE SEARCH

The next few moments were a blur of shouted voices and confusion in the dark. A woman—Samantha guessed it was Mrs. Billingsley—gave a piercing shriek.

"Someone get a light!" a man ordered.

"What the devil..." another man said angrily.

"The Blue Star!" Professor Wharton called out. "Where is it?"

There was a glimmer of light in the room. Samantha looked over and saw Mr. Jackson holding up a match. "Calm down, everyone," he said evenly. "No one's hurt, are they?"

"Of course nobody's hurt," snapped Mr. Billingsley. He pushed past Mr. Jackson and grabbed the bellpull. "Steward!" he yelled, yanking at the pull. He unlocked the door, opened it, and shouted down the hall. "Steward! Bring us a lamp!"

Mr. Jackson picked up the fallen candelabra and set it upright on the table. Two of the candles had rolled across the table, and Samantha replaced them in the candelabra. Mr. Jackson lit the candles, and a glow of light returned to the room. Samantha noticed that the jewel box had slid down toward her end of the table. Professor Wharton saw the box, too, and he reached for it eagerly. His hand fumbled a bit as he opened it.

Just then, a steward appeared at the door with a lit oil lamp. "You called for a lamp?" he inquired.

"Come in here and—" Mr. Billingsley began to order.

"NO!" the Professor barked. He turned toward the steward and Samantha saw that he was holding the open jewel box in his hand. "The Blue Star is gone," he reported, his voice trembling with emotion. "No one should enter or leave this room until it is found."

"Oh no!" cried Mrs. Billingsley. "It must have fallen out!" Holding her skirt with one hand, she glanced around the floor as if she expected the Blue Star to have rolled under her like a spool of thread.

Harry went to the doorway and took the lamp from the steward. "Bring two more lamps," he told the young man. "We may need them." As soon as the steward left, Harry closed and locked the door. The heavy click of the bolt made Samantha jump.

"Everyone stand here," ordered the Professor, directing the passengers toward a small area by the door. "Don't disturb anything by the table. My nephew and I will undertake a careful search of the room."

"I'll help," Mr. Jackson offered.

"No!" the Professor exclaimed. "Stay right where you are."

Does he suspect us of stealing the Blue Star? Samantha wondered. She swallowed hard, trying to fight back the growing tension she felt inside.

"This is an outrage!" fumed Mr. Billingsley, and Mrs. Billingsley and Charlotta nodded their agreement.

"My uncle is a trained archaeologist and I am his assistant," Harry explained. "If anyone can find the stone, we can. And it will be easier if only two people search. Otherwise, we'll all get in one another's way." He looked at them appealingly. "Please, just stand aside for a few minutes."

Mr. Billingsley grumbled, but everyone did as Harry requested. Samantha looked over at Nellie to see what she thought of the situation, but Nellie was staring at the floor as if it required all her attention.

Mr. Billingsley stood with his arms folded, his eyes narrowed to thin slits in his pudgy face. Both he and Mrs. Billingsley kept glancing toward Mademoiselle Étienne. Mademoiselle, however, had her eyes fixed on the Professor as he searched through the rumpled tablecloths, which had been pulled to the side of the table where Samantha had been sitting.

Harry crouched down under the big oak dining table and began to examine the floor there. Samantha wished she could help with the search. *I'm smaller,* she thought. *And I'm good at finding things.*

But the Professor and Harry clearly didn't want any help. So while they worked, Samantha and the other passengers looked on uneasily. Only Plato seemed happy. He busily swung from the porthole cover and then jumped to the floor next to Mrs. Billingsley. As Plato reached for the hem of Mrs. Billingsley's satin skirt, she shrieked, "Get away from me!"

Frightened, Plato retreated toward Samantha. He grabbed hold of her high-button boots, chattering wildly.

"It's all right," Samantha said, soothing the little monkey. She reached down and picked him up. He felt soft and warm in her arms, and his wide eyes looked up at her questioningly. "We're not going to hurt you."

"Good gracious, Plato!" said the Professor in exasperation. He had been hunched over examining a napkin that had fallen on the floor, but now he stood up, straightened his glasses, and gathered Plato from Samantha's arms. "I don't need you causing trouble right now," he told the monkey.

"You'd better make sure that wretched monkey doesn't have the sapphire," Mr. Billingsley called out.

The Professor carefully checked Plato's mouth and tiny hands and feet. "Plato is not holding anything," he reported.

A loud knock sounded at the door. When the Professor opened it, a steward was standing there with two more oil lamps. The Professor took the lamps and handed Plato to the steward. "Put him in his cage in my cabin, please," he directed the steward. "And bring another lamp or two, if you can."

Samantha watched anxiously as the

Professor carefully looked through all the napkins and then inspected both the lace table covering and the white linen tablecloth. Samantha felt sure that the sapphire would be found tucked somewhere inside the cloths. But the Professor found only crumbs.

Harry was on his hands and knees on the polished wood floor. He crawled under the table and looked under every chair. Samantha watched him collect a few pins, two pennies, a length of string, and a stray button. At last he shook his head sorrowfully. "I don't see it here."

Professor Wharton cradled his face in his hands for a moment, as if he were willing himself to wake up from a nightmare. Then he looked up at the other passengers. "Would you all please return to the seats you were in previously?" he asked in a hoarse voice. "We'll continue to search the rest of the room."

"I'm tired," Charlotta whined, "and I want to go to bed."

Samantha and Nellie glanced at each other.

We're tired, too, Samantha thought, *but we're not complaining.*

"You can't expect us to stay here forever, Professor," Mrs. Billingsley warned as she sat back at the table.

"We'll try to work as quickly as we can," Harry promised.

Harry and the Professor looked into every corner and under every surface of the small room. There were no carpets on the wood floors, and the only furniture, other than the dining table and chairs, was a single serving table. The search did not take too long. But all they discovered was another penny, a bent nail, and some dust balls.

"You said that bad luck comes to whoever carries the Blue Star," Mrs. Billingsley reminded the Professor. "Maybe this is proof of it. It seems as if the sapphire has disappeared."

"That's impossible, Madam," said the Professor, looking at her sternly. "I'm afraid that everyone must be searched."

"Searched!" exclaimed Mrs. Billingsley. Her plump face turned bright red. "Surely, sir, you wouldn't ask a lady to suffer such an indignity!"

Before Professor Wharton could answer, the dining-room door swung open and Captain Newman strode in, followed by the Admiral.

"So much for no one entering the room," Mr. Jackson murmured.

Captain Newman asked what was going on, and Professor Wharton explained the situation. Frowning, Captain Newman pulled out his pipe and asked to speak to the Professor outside. While the two men talked together in the hall, Samantha whispered to Nellie, "What will happen if they can't find the sapphire?"

"I don't know," Nellie whispered back, her face tight with worry.

A few minutes later, Captain Newman returned with the Professor. "The ladies," he said, bowing in the direction of Mrs. Billingsley, "may return to their cabins, but we ask that the gentlemen stay a while longer."

Mr. Billingsley turned on the Professor. "Are you accusing one of *us* of stealing your sapphire?"

"No one is being accused of anything," said Professor Wharton. "My nephew and I will be searched as well." He sat down heavily in one of the chairs, and Samantha saw that the color had drained from his face. "The Blue Star—the stone that I spent the last ten years of my life searching for—has somehow vanished from this room. It must be somewhere. I beseech all of you to help me find it."

Samantha saw Mr. and Mrs. Billingsley exchange a long look. Then Mr. Billingsley suddenly became agreeable. Sitting back in his chair, he told his wife and daughter that he would join them later. "I'm ready to stay here as long as you need me, Professor," he said as he folded his arms across his chest.

"Come, Charlotta," Mrs. Billingsley

directed. She and her daughter left the room together, followed by Samantha, Nellie, and Mademoiselle Étienne. As they walked down the steep stairs from the main deck to the first-class deck, Mrs. Billingsley said how foolish it had been for the Professor to take the sapphire out of its box. "He knew all along that the sapphire could bring bad luck," she complained. "I don't think it's wise to tempt fate, do you, Mademoiselle?"

Samantha fumed inwardly. She remembered how Mrs. Billingsley had urged the Professor to show them the sapphire. But she was silent.

Mademoiselle Étienne just shrugged. "Perhaps not, *Madame*," she replied.

When they reached the first-class deck, Charlotta, looking tired and sulky, hurried down the hallway toward the cabins. Mrs. Billingsley walked beside Mademoiselle Étienne, and Samantha and Nellie followed just behind them. Samantha was surprised to hear Mrs. Billingsley asking Mademoiselle Étienne about her teaching experience.

"I believe Mrs. Beemis mentioned that you recently worked for the Larchmont family in New York?"

"Oui, Madame," Mademoiselle Étienne answered politely, but she sounded cautious.

"And for how long?" Mrs. Billingsley persisted.

"Two years, *Madame.*"

"I see," said Mrs. Billingsley, seeming quite pleased by this answer. "Well, I know that the Larchmonts belong in the best New York society. Perhaps you would include my Charlotta in your French lessons during this trip? I would be happy to pay you, of course. Why don't you come to my cabin tomorrow to discuss it?"

"I would need to speak to Mrs. Beemis before we made such an arrangement, *Madame.*"

"Oh, I already talked with her about you," Mrs. Billingsley said with an airy wave. "I'm sure she wouldn't mind at all. In fact," she added, lowering her voice just a bit, "I think she'd be grateful that her granddaughter was associating with Charlotta."

Samantha's cheeks burned. She wondered whether Nellie had overheard Mrs. Billingsley's remark, too. But Nellie seemed lost in thought.

Once they entered their cabin, Samantha felt a rush of relief to be away from the Billingsleys. Mademoiselle Étienne, however, seemed uncharacteristically quiet. She said good night to the girls, and then, lighting another oil lamp, she took it and hurried to her room.

As soon as Samantha and Nellie were in their own room, Samantha whispered, "Do you think it was stolen?"

"Oh, Samantha, I hope not!" Nellie whispered back in a scared voice. By the light of their oil lamp, Nellie's face looked ashen. "I'm afraid it was, though—and I think the Professor suspects one of us."

Samantha nodded. As she and Nellie got ready for bed, she tried to imagine whether Mr. Billingsley or Mrs. Billingsley or Charlotta or Mr. Jackson or even Mademoiselle Étienne could be a thief. It was impossible, she decided. But if the sapphire hadn't been stolen, what had happened to it?

Lying in their berths, Samantha and Nellie talked in low tones about the evening's events, trying to think of any clues to the sapphire's whereabouts. "I didn't see *anything*," Nellie confessed. "I was trying to see the Blue Star when the room went dark and people started yelling. I never did get to see it."

"I know," Samantha sympathized. "Everything happened too fast." Yet the more she thought about the missing sapphire, the more Samantha felt as if she'd seen or heard something that might be a clue. She just couldn't remember what it was.

Maybe I'll think of it in the morning, she told herself as she dozed off.

She slept fitfully, though, and soon a rustling sound awakened her. It took her a minute to remember that she was aboard the ship instead of in her comfortable bed at home. She turned over in her bunk. By the faint moonlight coming through the porthole, Samantha saw the outline of Nellie in her white nightgown. She was standing a few feet away, in the doorway of their closet. Samantha heard the clunk of what sounded like a shoe landing on the closet floor.

"What are you doing?" Samantha asked groggily.

"Nothing," said Nellie. "I was having trouble sleeping, so I thought I'd tidy up some things."

Why is Nellie tidying her shoes in the middle of the night? Samantha wondered. But she was too tired to ask any more questions, and the rocking motion of the ship soon lulled her back to sleep.

6

A SUSPECT

In the morning, Samantha woke to the sound of a knock on the cabin's outer door. *Maybe they found the sapphire,* she thought excitedly as she threw on her dressing gown.

Sunlight was streaming in through the little porthole, and the sea was calm. "It's a beautiful day!" she told Nellie, who was still lying in bed, her blanket almost covering her face.

"I'll get up soon," Nellie promised, and then promptly rolled over in bed.

Samantha entered the cabin's parlor. At the same moment, Mademoiselle Étienne stepped out of her bedroom. She was wearing a navy skirt and fastening the buttons on the cuffs of her starched white shirtwaist.

"Bonjour, Mademoiselle," Samantha greeted

her. "I heard someone knock." Samantha opened the door and looked out. There was no one in the hallway, but she saw a square, cream-colored envelope that had been slid halfway under their door. She picked it up.

"I guess the steward delivered this," Samantha said, showing the envelope to Mademoiselle Étienne.

Mademoiselle Étienne looked at the initials written in large letters on the front: *N.E.* "Oh!" she exclaimed excitedly. "It's for me!"

Another knock sounded at the door. As Mademoiselle opened it, Samantha saw Oliver, their steward, standing in the hall. He bowed slightly and then announced in his most formal tone, "The Captain requests that the first-class passengers meet him at eight o'clock this morning in the saloon on the promenade deck."

"Thank you, Oliver," said Mademoiselle Étienne. She started to close the door, then stopped. Raising the envelope in her free hand, she added, "Oh, and thank you for delivering this."

Oliver looked puzzled. "Excuse me, Miss?"

"Didn't you put this under our door a few minutes ago?"

"No, Miss," said Oliver, shaking his head. "I didn't deliver anything."

"Ah, well, someone else must have brought it," Mademoiselle Étienne said with a shrug. She shut the door, and then quickly slit open the envelope with a look of happy anticipation on her face.

Samantha watched her, wondering if an invitation might be inside the envelope.

Mademoiselle Étienne pulled out a single sheet of cream-colored paper. As her eyes scanned the paper, she gasped and her face went white. Before Samantha could ask what was wrong, the tutor turned and rushed back into her bedroom, closing her door behind her.

Feeling increasingly uneasy, Samantha returned to Nellie, who was now sitting up in her berth. Samantha told her about the message from the Captain and described

Mademoiselle Étienne's strange reaction to her letter. "I wonder what's wrong."

"Maybe she was hoping for a message from her beau," Nellie suggested.

"Her beau?" Samantha echoed.

Nellie nodded. She explained that Mademoiselle wore a ring on a slender chain around her neck. "I noticed it when she and I were both sick and we were here in the cabin together. She told me that she'd been engaged to be married, but her beau's family hadn't approved of her."

"Why not?"

"He's a cousin of the Larchmonts, and his family is very rich. I guess they wanted him to marry someone rich, too. The engagement was ended and she said good-bye to her beau, but I think she's still in love with him." Nellie climbed out of bed and pulled on her robe. "Did Oliver say whether the Blue Star has been found?"

"No," Samantha admitted, wishing she had thought to ask the steward. *If the Blue Star had been found,* she wondered, *would the Captain be calling us all together at eight o'clock this morning?* Samantha looked at Nellie and knew that she was thinking the same thing.

"I'd better get up," Nellie said reluctantly.

By ten minutes to eight, Samantha and Nellie were dressed and ready to go to the saloon with Mademoiselle Étienne. The tutor was now neatly dressed in a navy blue jacket that matched her skirt, but her eyes were red, as if she'd been crying. As they walked up to the promenade deck, she continued the girls' lessons, pointing to objects and asking for their French names. "We must make good use of our time," she said with a jangle of her penny jar. "As soon as breakfast is over, we'll study verbs again, yes?"

When they arrived in the saloon, they found the Admiral and Grandmary already seated at a table along with Mr. and Mrs. Billingsley and Charlotta. Grandmary was working on her needlepoint, but she looked up as they took their chairs. "Good morning!

I hear you had a rather unpleasant evening last night. Perhaps everything will be settled this morning."

A moment later, Mr. Jackson, looking rumpled, hurried into the saloon together with Professor Wharton, who had dark circles under his eyes, and Harry, who was holding tight to Plato.

"So, Professor, any more developments since last night? Any clues to the disappearance?" Mr. Jackson asked eagerly. He held his pencil poised above a notebook, ready to write down the Professor's reply.

Samantha felt her stomach tighten as she waited for the answer, but Professor Wharton just waved the reporter aside. "Not now, Mr. Jackson. The Captain will be here soon and he'll explain everything."

Mr. Jackson took a seat beside Mademoiselle Étienne, greeting her with a friendly *"Bonjour!"* From across the table, Mrs. Billingsley looked at the reporter disapprovingly. He ran a hand over his unshaven chin. "Sorry about that," he said with a little laugh. "I was up late working on this story. Didn't quite have time to shave this morning."

Captain Newman entered exactly as the clock struck eight. Mr. Thatcher, his first mate, accompanied him. The passengers looked up expectantly as the Captain tapped his empty pipe in the palm of his hand and then delivered the grim news. "The dining room was searched thoroughly last night, but the Blue Star sapphire has not been found."

It must have been stolen! Samantha thought with a sick feeling. *But who would have done such a thing?*

The Captain tapped his pipe again, then said, "I apologize for the inconvenience, but it's necessary to search the rooms of all guests who were present when the box was opened. The crew also is being asked if they have seen anything suspicious."

"This is an insult to all of us," fumed Mrs. Billingsley.

Ignoring her protest, the Captain announced

that breakfast would be served in the saloon while he, Mr. Thatcher, Professor Wharton, and Harry searched the cabins. Captain Newman asked the Admiral if he would be willing to assist with the search, and the Admiral agreed. The other passengers were asked to remain in the saloon until the search was finished.

As the searchers left to begin their task, Samantha hoped that she'd put away all her dirty clothes. *Will they search those, too?* she wondered.

She looked around the table and saw that Mademoiselle Étienne was staring out the window, her eyebrows drawn together as if she was thinking about something very hard. Nellie was fidgeting nervously with her napkin. *Everyone's worried,* Samantha realized. Then she glanced at Mr. Jackson and saw that he was grinning as he checked his watch. *Well, almost everyone,* she decided.

"The search began at eight-fifteen," Mr. Jackson announced gleefully, and he started scribbling away with his pencil.

"What are you so pleased about?" asked Mrs. Billingsley acidly. "Surely, you're not happy to hear the news that the Blue Star is still missing."

"I'm a reporter, ma'am, and news is my business," Mr. Jackson replied. He put out his hands as if framing an imaginary headline. "'Bad Luck Follows Blue Star Across Sea'— that story will sell papers, don't you think?"

Instead of replying, Mrs. Billingsley turned to the other passengers at the table and sniffed, "It seems that virtually *anyone* is allowed to travel first class these days, even people who are clearly not of the best society. It seems to me that if a crime has been committed, *those* people"—and here she looked directly at Mr. Jackson—"should be searched first."

Samantha shifted uneasily in her chair. But Mr. Jackson stroked his stubbly chin and said calmly, "Perhaps you are forgetting that all the *men* who attended the dinner last night were searched. Even the monkey was checked.

A Suspect

So only one of the *ladies* could have carried the sapphire out of the room." Mr. Jackson stood up. "Now if you'll excuse me, I'll go work on my story."

Mrs. Billingsley watched him walk away with a thoughtful expression on her face. Then she turned to Grandmary and said in a loud voice, "You know, Mrs. Beemis, I've wanted to mention to you how unwise it is to allow the help to dine with first-class passengers. I know some people treat their children's tutors as members of the family, but in my opinion that is a tremendous mistake."

Grandmary always sat with perfect posture, but Samantha now saw her spine stiffen even further. "Really, Mrs. Billingsley?" she said icily. "If you are referring to Mademoiselle Étienne, let me assure you that she is a very well-bred young lady, and, as I believe I have already told you, she came to us highly recommended from the Larchmonts."

"Ah, yes, the Larchmonts!" Mrs. Billingsley smiled triumphantly at Mademoiselle Étienne.

"I do remember you mentioning them. But I also remember that their house in Southhampton was robbed only last month. Some very valuable items were taken. I saw several articles about it in the papers."

So that's why Mrs. Billingsley asked about the Larchmonts last night, Samantha realized. *She suspects Mademoiselle Étienne is the thief!*

Samantha looked over and saw that Mademoiselle Étienne's slender hands were gripping the table so tightly that her knuckles were white. "*Madame,* the house that was robbed was the summer home of the Larchmonts, and it was empty at the time," the tutor told Mrs. Billingsley. "The Larchmont family was in New York City and I was with them."

Mrs. Billingsley arched her eyebrows. "Well, as far as I know, they haven't caught the thief yet—*whoever* it is."

Grandmary stood up with great dignity. "You must excuse me, Mrs. Billingsley, but I believe that the light at that table will be better for my needlework," she said, nodding toward a table at the farthest end of the saloon. She picked up her needlepoint. "Mademoiselle Étienne, perhaps you and the girls will accompany me and work on your French lessons over there?"

Samantha followed her grandmother, Nellie, and Mademoiselle Étienne to the far table. She knew that Grandmary believed firmly that a lady should never be rude to the "help." *Maybe now Grandmary will realize that the Billingsleys aren't very nice*, Samantha thought with relief.

Sun sparkled in through the saloon's windows as the stewards served a breakfast of ham, lamb chops, scrambled eggs, and muffins. The food looked delicious, but Samantha was too nervous to eat more than half a muffin. As soon as the dishes were cleared, Mademoiselle Étienne began quizzing Samantha and Nellie on their verbs while Grandmary worked on her needlepoint.

Samantha tried to concentrate on her lesson, but she kept hoping for some sign of the searchers. Mademoiselle Étienne had almost filled up the lesson jar with pennies when Captain Newman and the other men returned to the saloon. Samantha knew by the stern look on the Captain's face that the news wasn't good. She glanced at the Admiral and saw that he looked worried, too.

"Did you find something?" Mr. Jackson asked as all the first-class passengers gathered around the Captain.

"Not exactly," Captain Newman admitted. He turned to Mademoiselle Étienne. "One of the crew says that something was thrown from your porthole this morning, shortly before our meeting. What did you throw away?"

Mademoiselle looked startled. "Why does he think it was my window?"

"He has been with the ship several years," the Captain explained. "He knows which porthole belongs to which cabin. And he saw an arm wearing a blue sleeve with a white cuff. I believe that describes you, Mademoiselle."

Everyone turned to look at Mademoiselle

Étienne. The cuffs of her white shirtwaist extended below the sleeves of her navy blue jacket. She returned the other passengers' stares for a moment, and then she lowered her head. "Very well, I did throw something," she admitted. "But it was only a piece of paper, nothing of importance!"

Samantha and Nellie looked at each other. *Could Mademoiselle be hiding something?* Samantha wondered in disbelief.

"Please, speak frankly," the Admiral urged in a kindly tone as he pulled out a chair for Mademoiselle. "We're only trying to understand what happened."

Mademoiselle Étienne sat down, and then she looked up at the gathered passengers like a wounded bird gazing at a pack of hunting dogs.

"Everyone, please sit down," said the Captain, taking a seat himself. "Now, Miss Étienne, why did you throw the paper out the porthole?"

Mademoiselle Étienne took a deep breath.

Then in a low voice she said that someone had put an envelope under the door of Cabin 7. The envelope had been addressed to her.

Samantha tried to get the Captain's attention. She wanted to say that she had seen the envelope, too. "Excuse me," she began.

Captain Newman shook his head. "Not now," he told Samantha. Then he nodded at Mademoiselle Étienne and asked her to continue her story. The tutor said that she had opened the envelope and had discovered a note accusing her of stealing the sapphire.

"But it's not true—I didn't steal anything," Mademoiselle Étienne protested. She explained that she had been so angry that she had thrown the note into the ocean.

"You do believe me, don't you?" she asked, looking at the faces around her.

"Yes, of course!" Nellie blurted out. But Samantha was silent. She wasn't sure what to believe.

7
MONKEY BUSINESS?

For a moment, no one in the saloon spoke. Then the Captain cleared his throat. "Miss Étienne, I would like to discuss this with you further. Please come with me."

The Admiral and Grandmary stood up as well. "We'll come, too," the Admiral offered.

"Yes," agreed Grandmary, standing ramrod straight. "Mademoiselle Étienne is a member of our party."

Grandmary walked out of the room side by side with Mademoiselle Étienne, and the Admiral and Captain Newman followed close behind. After they left, Mr. Thatcher said that the other passengers could return to their cabins.

Nellie half-ran down the stairs and through the corridors. Samantha had to race to keep up with her. As soon as their door was closed behind them, Nellie threw herself on her berth. "It's not fair!" she cried. "It's not fair! She didn't do anything wrong!"

Samantha hesitated. She liked Mademoiselle Étienne and she believed her story about the envelope. But the sapphire *had* disappeared. "I don't think that Mademoiselle stole the Blue Star," she said to Nellie, "but it's possible."

"No," Nellie argued. "She wouldn't do something like that. She's a good person. When I was sick, she sat and talked with me to cheer me up." Nellie wiped her eyes. "Did you know that she's an orphan—like you and me? Her grandfather brought her up."

Samantha nodded. She remembered the portrait of the elderly gentleman and how fondly Mademoiselle had spoken of him. She wanted to believe that the French tutor was everything she seemed—a kind young woman who missed her grandfather and was looking forward to returning to him.

But Samantha also remembered the pressed

flower next to Mademoiselle Étienne's bed. She told Nellie about it. "I think her beau gave her the rose," Samantha concluded.

"Probably," Nellie said. "They were in love."

"What if Mademoiselle is *still* in love with him?" Samantha suggested. "What if she still hopes to marry him?"

"His family won't let him marry her because she's not rich," Nellie reminded her.

Samantha stared silently at her hands. She didn't want to mention her terrible thought— but Nellie guessed it. "You think Mademoiselle might have taken the sapphire so that she'd be rich and her beau could marry her," Nellie exclaimed. "But you're wrong!"

"I don't want to think that she's the thief," said Samantha. "But one of the people in the dining room last night *must* have stolen it."

Nellie stood up and began pacing the length of the small cabin. She could take only three or four steps at a time before turning around, but she was so lost in thought that she didn't seem to notice. "Maybe not!" she said at last. "Remember when Mrs. Van Sicklen thought I'd taken her pearls?"

Samantha nodded. That had happened when Nellie was a servant for Grandmary's neighbors, the Van Sicklen family.

"You knew I wasn't a thief, so we looked for the pearls together—and we solved the mystery," Nellie recalled. "Well, I know that Mademoiselle Étienne never would have stolen the Blue Star, so why don't you and I go look for it together? Maybe it's still somewhere in the dining room."

Samantha felt nervous about searching the Captain's private dining room. "What if one of the stewards comes in and finds us?"

"We'll make sure no one is around," Nellie said confidently.

"Let's wait and talk to Mademoiselle Étienne first," Samantha suggested. "Maybe it will turn out that she's not a suspect after all. I'm sure she'll be back here after lunch."

Nellie agreed with this plan. But lunch came and went and there was no sign of Mademoiselle

Monkey Business?

Étienne. The afternoon passed slowly. While Nellie worked on her arithmetic problems, Samantha began her French essay. She could hardly write a single phrase. She kept glancing up at the door, hoping Mademoiselle Étienne would walk in any minute.

Finally the door opened. It was Doris. "Mrs. Beemis asked me to pack up the French girl's things," she told them.

"Why?" Samantha asked loudly.

Doris shrugged. "Don't know. She's moving to another cabin. I'll be taking her place here."

As soon as Doris left the cabin, Samantha and Nellie exchanged a long look. Samantha nodded. "Let's go," she said in a low tone.

Together, they made their way up to the Captain's dining room. They peeked inside and saw that a steward was in the room. He was busy arranging clean tablecloths on the dining table, and he didn't notice the girls. They hurried by.

"Where do we go now?" Samantha whispered.

"Maybe we could walk up to the saloon and wait there," suggested Nellie.

"As long as Charlotta's not there," said Samantha.

The girls climbed the stairs to the promenade deck and then ventured out on the open passageway. The sky had turned cloudy and the wind was whipping at the waves. Samantha held tightly to her skirt and hurried down the passageway, trying not to imagine what it would be like to fall into that cold seawater.

When they reached the door of the saloon, Nellie opened it a crack. Both girls saw Charlotta reading in an armchair. Nellie quickly closed the door. "Let's try the dining room again," she suggested.

By the time they returned to the dining room, the steward had gone. The girls quietly slipped inside. The room was shadowy, and only dim light shone through the portholes. "We should have brought an oil lamp," said Samantha.

Nellie smiled. "I brought matches!" she said. She pulled them from her pocket and lit the candles on the candelabra.

Samantha looked around the room uneasily. "I hope no one catches us in here."

Nellie nodded. "We'll have to hurry."

The only furniture in the room was the round dining table, the ten chairs that surrounded it, two extra chairs by the wall, and a long serving table where dishes were kept hot during dinner. Now, however, the serving table was cleared of dishes, and there was nothing on the dining table but the tablecloths and the candelabra.

Samantha remembered that the Professor and Harry had not spent much time looking at the serving table, so she carefully ran her hands under and over it. All she found was a wine cork that had become wedged against the wall. Nellie, meanwhile, picked up each chair and looked under and around it.

"Nothing!" she reported gloomily after she put down the last chair.

Next, the girls got down on their knees and started to search the floor, running their hands carefully along the cracks between the floorboards. Samantha discovered a small button behind the door, and Nellie found a sewing pin hidden in a crack.

"There's some dust here," Nellie reported as she searched under the table. "Oh, look, here's another pin."

"Do you see any cracks big enough to hold the sapphire?" Samantha asked as she crawled under the table, too.

"Not yet," admitted Nellie. "But it's hard to see and—"

Just then, the dining-room door opened and there was the sound of footsteps entering the room. Both girls froze. Samantha felt her heart beating hard in her chest. *How can we explain to the steward why we're under here?*

The footsteps drew nearer, and someone lifted up the tablecloth. Samantha saw the grinning face of Jack Jackson peering down at her. "I don't think you'll find the sapphire under there," he said. "I've already looked myself. Why don't you come out?"

Feeling a little silly, Samantha crawled out from under the table, and Nellie quickly followed her.

"How did you know we were under there?" Samantha asked.

"I've been looking for you girls," he confessed. "When I couldn't find you in your cabin or in the saloon or walking the decks, I thought I'd try in here."

"Why were you looking for us, Mr. Jackson?" asked Nellie.

"Call me Jack," he said. "Everyone does." He pulled a notebook from his jacket pocket. Leaning against the table, he explained that he was writing a story on the theft of the Blue Star. "I wanted to talk to you girls about last night."

He proceeded to ask exactly where they had been when the candelabra fell and what they had heard and seen. He jotted down their answers with the stub of a pencil. Then he narrowed his eyes slightly. "Miss Étienne was sitting between you girls when the candelabra fell—did you notice what she did?"

Nellie bristled. "She didn't do anything."

Jack fingered his pencil thoughtfully. "Maybe not," he agreed. "But the sapphire's not here, and it didn't fly away on its own. One of the people at the table must've grabbed it. Who do you think it was?"

Samantha tried to think back and remember everyone who had been sitting around the dining table. She had a sudden, vivid picture of all the passengers enjoying their dinner while Plato scampered about the room, grabbing everything that caught his eye. Suddenly, she had an idea. "Maybe it wasn't any of us!" she exclaimed. "The Professor's monkey, Plato, has little hands. He could've reached into the box and taken the sapphire."

"But the Professor checked his hands—and his mouth, too," Nellie objected.

"Plato could have hidden the sapphire somewhere *before* the Professor searched him," Samantha persisted.

Monkey Business?

Jack looked at her skeptically. "I considered that theory," he admitted. "I could just see the headlines: *'MONKEY STEALS BLUE STAR SAPPHIRE!'*" He sighed. "It would've been a great story."

"But it's possible!" protested Samantha.

"In a dime-store novel, maybe," allowed Jack. "But do you really think that little monkey could've climbed across the table, grabbed the sapphire in the dark, and then hidden it somewhere where no one's been able to find it—all in about a minute?"

"What if he was trained to do it?" Samantha suggested. "I've seen organ grinders' monkeys, and they do all sorts of tricks."

Samantha looked at Nellie for support, but Nellie shook her head. "The organ grinder I knew said that it takes a long time to train a monkey. Months, maybe even years. The Professor has only had Plato for a month or so. And why would he train a monkey to steal his own sapphire?"

Samantha glanced around the room, and

the portholes caught her eye. "What if Plato wasn't trained—maybe he just took the sapphire and threw it out the window? That would explain why we can't find it."

Jack shrugged. "I suppose it's possible. But I don't believe it. And I don't think my editors would, either. Besides, there's another problem. Here, I'll show you."

He asked the girls to sit in the same chairs they had been in the previous night. Then he positioned himself at the other side of the round table, where the Professor had stood. "What happened to the tablecloth?" he asked.

"It slid down this way," Samantha told him. "Into my lap."

"That's right," Jack agreed. "And nobody—person or monkey—could've *pushed* the cloth across the table like that. Not without everybody noticing, anyway. It had to have been *pulled* from that direction. So someone on *your* side of the table must have pulled it."

Jack pointed at the chairs as if each were occupied. "Either you, Samantha, or you,

Nellie, or Miss Étienne, or—and this would have been harder, but possible—me or that blond girl, the Billingsleys' daughter."

"Charlotta," Samantha filled in for him.

"Yes, Charlotta," said Jack. He looked at the table thoughtfully, as if trying to re-create the theft in his mind. "I know I didn't steal the sapphire, so unless one of you girls has taken to crime at a young age, my money is on Miss Étienne. If you could prove me wrong, though, I wouldn't be sorry. She seems like a nice kid."

Nellie stood up. Samantha looked at her and saw that all the color had vanished from her face. "Mademoiselle Étienne *is* nice and she didn't steal anything," Nellie declared. Then she rushed out of the dining room.

Jack watched Nellie go. "She seems very sure that Miss Étienne is innocent," he said softly, almost as if he were speaking to himself.

"We're both sure," Samantha agreed. She tried to sound more confident than she felt, but inside she wondered, *Is Mademoiselle really a thief?*

8
HIDDEN

Feeling very confused, Samantha decided
to go talk to Grandmary and the Admiral.
Just as she was about to knock on their door,
Doris stepped out of the cabin carrying a
basket of folded laundry under her arm. "If
you're looking for your grandmother, she's
gone to the promenade deck for a breath of
fresh air," the maid reported loudly.

"Oh," said Samantha, disappointed. Then
the Admiral's voice came from inside the
cabin. "Come in, Samantha!" he called. "I
would like to have a word with you."

As Doris briskly carried the laundry down
the hall, Samantha entered her grandparents'
cabin. The Admiral was sitting at the table
with a book, and he looked up at her with

concern. "How are you?" he asked. "Not too upset by the recent events, I hope?"

"Nellie and I have been wondering where Mademoiselle Étienne is," Samantha said as she sat down. "We haven't even seen her since this morning. Doris said she's been moved to some other cabin."

The Admiral put down his book. "Under the circumstances, we thought it would be best if Mademoiselle Étienne moved into another cabin in first class," he said gravely. "She's now in Cabin 32."

In the back of her mind, Samantha had worried that Mademoiselle might have been thrown into a jail cell in the depths of the ship, getting only bread and water for meals. She was relieved that Mademoiselle was in a first-class cabin instead. Samantha explained to the Admiral that Mademoiselle Étienne had been telling the truth when she said that a note had been delivered to their cabin. "I saw it myself. Someone put it under our door."

"Did you read the message?" he asked.

"No," Samantha admitted. "I only saw the envelope. But the note made Mademoiselle very upset. I think she was crying."

The Admiral promised to tell Captain Newman what Samantha had seen. Then he looked solemn. "The Captain and I have spent quite a bit of time discussing the sapphire's disappearance. He recognizes that there is no *proof* of guilt against Mademoiselle Étienne."

"May Nellie and I still take French lessons?"

"No," said the Admiral, shaking his head. "Mademoiselle Étienne will remain in her own cabin and there will be no more lessons. This is a serious matter, Samantha. Although there is no proof that Mademoiselle Étienne committed the crime, there is reason to think that she may have been involved. And, under the circumstances, your grandmother and I wish to be cautious. Do you understand?"

Samantha dropped her eyes under the Admiral's stern gaze. "What will happen to Mademoiselle?"

"She will be questioned by the authorities

when the ship arrives in London," he explained. "Until then, the search for the sapphire has been called off. The Captain suspects that the thief may have become scared and thrown the sapphire overboard. Or the thief may have someone working with him—or her—and have hidden the sapphire in a place we wouldn't guess. The Captain says it would be pointless to disrupt the ship with any further searches."

The Admiral relaxed in his chair and smiled slightly. "To tell the truth, I think Captain Newman is a bit annoyed that the Professor didn't put the sapphire in the ship's safe so that no one would have been tempted by it."

Just then, Grandmary returned to the cabin, her cheeks pink from the cold. "I'm glad to see you, dear," she told Samantha. "I realize this unfortunate incident must be difficult for you and Nellie."

"We're worried about Mademoiselle Étienne," Samantha confessed. She looked up at her grandmother. "You don't really think that she stole the sapphire, do you?"

Samantha saw her grandparents exchange a long look. "We hope not," Grandmary said finally. "Yet we may never know for sure."

We may never know for sure. Samantha thought about Grandmary's words as she returned to her cabin. She wanted to talk with Nellie, but the cabin was empty. *Where can she be?* Samantha wondered. *In the saloon?*

While she waited for Nellie to return, Samantha curled up on the top bunk with her doll Clara and tried to read by the light of the porthole. As she turned the pages of *Treasure Island,* she discovered that a character she'd liked couldn't really be trusted. *Is anyone what they seem to be?* she wondered.

She heard the cabin door open and someone enter the parlor. For a moment, she thought Nellie had returned, but then there was a sharp knock at her bedroom door. Doris came in, carrying two pairs of high-button boots. "I blacked these so they'd be ready for you and Nellie to wear to dinner tonight," Doris announced.

"Thank you," said Samantha as Doris deposited the boots on the floor of the closet.

"Eh?"

"THANK YOU!" Samantha repeated.

Doris nodded. "I'll go light the oil lamps," she added as she left. "Your dresses are in the closet. You and Nellie had better get ready for dinner. The Admiral and Mrs. Beemis will be fetching you soon."

Reluctantly, Samantha climbed down from her bed and put on her velvet dress with its crisply starched linen collar. Then she looked at the two pairs of almost identical boots in the closet. She and Nellie had kept their boots on opposite sides of the closet. Now that Doris had rearranged them, Samantha wasn't sure which boots were hers. She knew her feet were slightly larger than Nellie's, so she chose the two boots that looked biggest. The boot she pulled onto her right foot fit perfectly, but the left boot felt strange, as if something was caught under the sole.

Samantha took off the boot and peered

inside. An edge of paper peeked out from under the lining. Puzzled, she reached in and pulled out the paper. It was a ten-dollar bill.

"Jiminy!" Samantha whispered to herself. She peered further into the boot and found a five-dollar bill. It was folded and tucked away between the lining and the sole.

Her heart pounding, Samantha ran her hand inside the other boots. In one, she found three more five-dollar bills. All together, she counted thirty dollars. Samantha sat back for a moment, stunned. How could Nellie have so much money? Their allowance was a dime a week. Even if Nellie had saved every penny, she couldn't possibly have collected thirty dollars!

And why had Nellie put the money in her boots? Samantha suddenly remembered how Nellie had been awake in the middle of the night, doing something near the closet.

She was hiding money! thought Samantha, stunned. *But why? And where did she get it?*

9

LETTERS HOME

Samantha was sitting on the floor, staring at the money, when she heard the cabin's outer door open. Quickly, she began stuffing the bills back inside the boots. Before she could finish, Nellie walked in.

Nellie looked down at her in shocked silence.

"I . . . I was putting on my boots and I . . ." Samantha tried to stammer an explanation, but she found herself at a loss for words. "I . . . I found these." She gestured at the folded bills.

"You were looking through my things." Nellie spoke softly.

"I didn't mean to! It was an accident," Samantha protested. "But . . . but where did all this money come from?"

Nellie got down on the floor and started fitting the money back into the boots. "If I told you, you wouldn't believe me," she said quietly. "Just like no one believes Mademoiselle Étienne." Nellie pursed her lips together—as if she had nothing more to say—and she refused to let her eyes meet Samantha's.

Samantha swallowed hard. She and Nellie had been through so many hard times together. *Why won't she explain this money? Doesn't she trust me?*

Both girls heard Doris enter the parlor. "The Admiral and Mrs. Beemis will be here any minute, girls," Doris called out loudly.

Without a word, Samantha and Nellie worked together to quickly hide the bills back inside the boots' linings. As soon as they were done, Nellie turned away. "You won't tell anyone about the money, will you?" she asked in a tight voice.

Does she really think I would? Samantha wondered. "No, I won't," she told Nellie stiffly, and then added, "You had better get dressed for dinner."

"Please apologize to the Admiral and your grandmother for me," Nellie said, her back still turned to Samantha. "I'm not going to dinner."

Why? Samantha wanted to ask. All she said was, "All right."

That night at dinner, Samantha wished with all her heart that Nellie and Mademoiselle Étienne were there beside her. Most of the other people at the table talked together in small groups. As the eldest lady present, Grandmary now sat in the place of honor next to Captain Newman, and she and the Admiral chatted with him about their experiences at sea. Professor Wharton sat next to Samantha, and she saw that behind his glasses, his eyes were rimmed with dark circles.

Samantha searched for something to say to him. Finally, she said quietly, "I'm very sorry about the Blue Star."

"Thank you, my dear," he said, patting her hand absentmindedly. "I blame myself for its loss. I should have learned by now that greed can overcome even good people." He shook his head forlornly. "I'll never forgive myself for my carelessness."

The Professor hardly spoke for the rest of the meal, and Samantha was forced to listen to Charlotta brag about her sister's upcoming marriage to a French count.

"How nice," Samantha murmured occasionally. Her thoughts, however, kept returning to Nellie. Why had she refused to come to dinner? Was she going somewhere else instead? And—most puzzling of all— why wouldn't she say where all that money came from?

We'll talk together tonight, Samantha promised herself. Yet by the time Samantha returned from the long dinner, Nellie was already in bed asleep—or pretending to sleep.

"Nellie?" Samantha whispered hopefully. "Are you awake?" But there was no answer.

The next day, Nellie continued to avoid Samantha. She spoke only when necessary,

and then with a chilly politeness that, to
Samantha, felt worse than anger. The only
thing good about the day, as far as Samantha
was concerned, was that the electrical
generator finally began working again.

After lunch the two girls read silently
in their cabin. Samantha felt very much alone.
As she turned the pages of *Treasure Island*, she
found herself thinking about other treasures:
the missing sapphire and Nellie's mysteriously
hidden money.

There is no connection between the two,
Samantha told herself. *Nellie would never, ever
steal something or help anyone to steal.*

But doubts gathered inside her mind like
mosquito bites demanding to be scratched. *If
Nellie hasn't done anything wrong, why does she
look so worried? And why won't she talk to me?*

Samantha finally decided to get some fresh
air. "I'm going for a walk," she told Nellie.
"Would you like to come?"

Nellie did not even look up from her book.
"No, thank you."

Samantha put on her coat and walked up to the promenade deck. There was a glimmer of sun in the sky, but the icy wind cut through her coat. After two turns about the deck, she decided to visit the saloon. There she found a cheerful fire in the coal-burning stove and several passengers sitting at the small tables, writing letters. The room was quiet except for the scratching of pen against paper. Jack was sitting at a table near the door, and he looked up when Samantha came in. "Hello!" he said, speaking softly. "Have you come to write letters, too?"

"Is that what everyone else is doing?"

"Not me," said Jack with a smile. He glanced down at the scribbling on his notepad. "I'm working on my story, 'Blue Star Mysteriously Disappears.' I hope to be able to telegraph it back to New York when we get to land. But I think the others are writing letters—you know we can post them from Queenstown tomorrow, when we dock on the coast of Ireland."

Samantha glanced around the room.

Mrs. Billingsley was writing notes on cream-colored stationery, and Harry looked as if he was doing business correspondence. "Maybe I'll write my letters, too," she told Jack.

"If you remember anything about the Blue Star's theft, let me know," Jack said with a wink.

Samantha nodded and found an empty table. The steward offered her a pen and ink along with special stationery that said "R.M.S. *Queen Caroline*" at the top. She filled the pen with ink and wrote, *Dear Bridget and Jenny, How are you?*

Then she stopped. She wasn't sure what to write next. She couldn't exactly say that she was fine. But how could she tell Bridget and Jenny about the events of the trip without worrying them? She tore up her first note, and then tried a second and tore that up, too. For the third time, she wrote, *Dear Bridget and Jenny.* Then she sat staring at the blank page.

A voice came from behind her. "Haven't written much, have you?"

Startled, Samantha turned around and saw Charlotta peering over her shoulder. "No, not yet," Samantha admitted.

"Let's play checkers," Charlotta suggested.

Samantha looked down at her unfinished letter. *Anything would be better than this*, she decided. "All right."

They moved to another table where Charlotta set up the black and red checkers with the quick precision of an expert. She put the black pieces on her side of the board, giving Samantha the red. "'Coal before fire,'" Charlotta announced as she prepared to make the first move.

Just then, Nellie came into the saloon. She glanced quickly around the room and then headed for the table where Samantha and Charlotta were sitting. "Samantha, I want to—" Nellie began in a quiet voice.

Samantha looked up hopefully, but before Nellie could finish her sentence, Charlotta interrupted. "Can't you see we're playing a game together?" she demanded.

For a moment, anger blazed in Nellie's eyes, and Samantha was sure she was going to say something. Then Nellie bit her lip and turned away without another word.

"Goodness, some people have no manners!" Charlotta complained loudly as Nellie walked away. Then she nodded to Samantha. "Your move."

Samantha played quickly. She wanted to finish the game so that she could go and talk with Nellie. Charlotta, however, slowly considered every move she made. As she played, she continued to chatter, offering Samantha advice on everything from checkers ("That was a silly move!") to clothes ("Would you like to borrow my magazines so you can see the new styles?")

Finally, Charlotta brought up the subject of friends. "You really shouldn't associate with inferior people, Samantha," she advised as she captured another red checker. "After all," she added, lowering her voice to a whisper, "how do you know that Nellie didn't help

Mademoiselle Étienne steal the sapphire? Nellie used to be a servant, didn't she? Everyone knows that servants steal."

Samantha felt the blood rise to her cheeks. How could Charlotta suspect Nellie of such a thing? And worse still, how could she herself have ever doubted Nellie—even for a moment? Samantha suddenly realized how foolish she had been. She stood up, trembling with anger.

"Nellie is my sister *and* my best friend!" she told Charlotta. "She's never stolen anything in her life. And if you say she has... well, then you're the inferior person, Charlotta Billingsley!" As Samantha turned away, her swirling skirt hit the checkerboard and scattered the red and black pieces all over the floor. But she didn't care. She rushed out of the saloon, past Mrs. Billingsley, who was staring at her with shocked disapproval, and past Jack, who was smiling gleefully.

Samantha had something to say to Nellie. And she knew it couldn't wait.

10

A QUESTION OF IDENTITY

Samantha hurried to their cabin, where she found Nellie sitting at the small table in the parlor. "Nellie," she began breathlessly, "I don't care what you think, I wasn't spying on you. Doris had just blacked the boots and I got them mixed up. And I know you'd never steal anything—"

"I know, Samantha," Nellie interrupted. Her voice was quivering. She stood up from the table. "You're the best friend I've ever had. I'm sorry I got so angry. I felt like you suspected me, just like everyone suspects Mademoiselle Étienne. And I can explain about the money."

"You don't have to explain," Samantha assured her.

Nellie gave a half smile. "I want to." Then

she lowered her voice. "But I don't want anyone to hear us. Let's go into the other room."

They both sat down on Nellie's berth. "Remember the boy who stopped us after school the day before we left on the trip?" Nellie asked.

"Yes," Samantha said slowly. "His name was Jamie, wasn't it?"

Nellie nodded, and for a moment she stared down at the red blanket on her bed. "I kept a secret from you that afternoon," she said finally. "What Jamie wanted was for me to take a packet of money with me on this trip and send it by post once we reached Queenstown. Jamie's cousin, Rory, is still in Ireland. Jamie had promised to send money so that Rory could come to America."

"Why didn't Jamie mail the money from New York himself?"

Nellie continued to stare down at the blanket. "He doesn't trust the post office. He said he'd tried mailing money once before, but it never reached his cousin." Nellie looked up searchingly into Samantha's face. "I didn't *want* to do this for Jamie. But I couldn't tell him no, not after everything his father did to help my father."

Samantha thought for a moment. "But why didn't you tell me?"

Nellie looked embarrassed. "After what the policeman said about Jamie, I thought you'd be ashamed to have anything to do with him. So I didn't want to tell you that I'd agreed to help him."

"Is that why you hid the money in your boots?"

"No," Nellie said. "I only put it there after the Blue Star disappeared. I was pretty sure they would search the ship. I was afraid that if they found the money in my trunk, they'd suspect *me* of stealing, just like they suspect Mademoiselle Étienne. My mam always said that the safest place for money is in your boot, so I hid it there." Nellie smiled. "Mam never would have guessed that someone like Doris would take my boots away to black them!"

Both girls laughed. Then Nellie looked serious again. She confided to Samantha that she didn't know how to mail Jamie's money once the ship docked at Queenstown. "And," Nellie added, looking very serious, "we have to think of a way to help Mademoiselle Étienne."

"The Admiral will know how to send the money. We'll ask him to help us," Samantha said confidently. "And he told me that Mademoiselle Étienne may be questioned in London, but there's no proof against her."

"I looked for her last night—while you were at dinner," Nellie said. "It took me a while to find her cabin, but then I heard someone crying and I knew I'd reached the right one. When she opened the door, she told me she was fine, but I know she's upset. How will she ever get another job if there are rumors that she's a thief? Even if it's not proven?"

Samantha was silent for a few minutes. The thought of Mademoiselle Étienne crying alone in her cabin was more than she could bear. Finally, she looked up at Nellie. "If the thief wasn't Mademoiselle or Plato, somebody else in the dining room must have stolen the sapphire. Let's write a list of everyone who was there."

Nellie dug out a few sheets of lined paper from her schoolbooks, and Samantha found a pencil. At the top of the list, Nellie wrote:

1. *Professor Wharton—He was the one actually holding the sapphire.* ("He doesn't make any sense," Samantha protested. "Why would he steal from himself?" "We have to include everyone," Nellie insisted.)

2. *Harry—He was sitting right next to the Professor.* ("Do you really think he'd steal from his own uncle?" Samantha asked. She had started to wonder whether the list was a silly idea. "Maybe," Nellie said defensively. "We can't be sure.")

3. *Mr. Billingsley—He wanted the sapphire for his collection.* ("He tried to buy the

sapphire from the Professor, but the Professor wouldn't even consider it," Samantha recalled.)

4. *Mrs. Billingsley—She loves jewels.* ("She was the one who begged the Professor to bring out the sapphire again," Samantha added. "You're right," said Nellie thoughtfully.)

5. *Charlotta—She could have pulled the tablecloth.* ("She probably didn't steal the sapphire herself," Nellie admitted, "but she might've helped her parents.")

6. *Jack Jackson—He wants an exciting story for his newspaper.* ("And maybe he needs money, too," Nellie suggested.)

7. *Mademoiselle Étienne—She was sitting in the right place.* ("Also, someone sent her a note saying that she was the thief," Samantha pointed out.)

"*Any* of them could have taken the sapphire," Nellie said as she reread the list. "Maybe the thief just wrote the note so that people would suspect Mademoiselle Étienne."

Samantha looked at the list, too. She noticed Nellie's neat round handwriting, so different from her own. Suddenly she had an idea. "We might be able to find out who wrote the note to Mademoiselle Étienne."

"How?"

Samantha told her about all the passengers she had seen writing letters in the saloon. "Maybe some of them made mistakes and threw away letters, like I did. If we can get their letters out of the trash, Mademoiselle Étienne might recognize someone's handwriting."

Nellie's eyes brightened. "Let's hurry!"

The girls put on their coats and walked quickly up to the saloon. Its wide windows offered a clear view of the seemingly endless horizon. Dark clouds were gathering in the distance, but the setting sun tinted the sky with purple and blue. Fortunately, however, no passengers had stayed to admire the sunset. The room was empty, so Samantha and Nellie went straight to the trash baskets and picked out all the crumpled pieces of paper they could find. They stuffed the papers into the pockets of their coats and hurried back to their cabin.

Inside the cabin, they found Doris tidying up the little parlor. Samantha and Nellie quickly retreated to their bedroom. There they spread the papers on the lower berth and sorted through them. There was a rough draft of a story written by Jack Jackson, an ink-splattered letter to the British Museum written by Harry Wharton, and a torn-up note written by Professor Wharton. What Samantha found most interesting of all, though, was a cream-colored envelope. The Billingsleys' return address was written on the back in a woman's handwriting. On the front, another address had been written and then crossed out.

Samantha picked up the envelope and examined it carefully. "This is the same kind of envelope that the note was in. And this must be Mrs. Billingsley's handwriting."

A QUESTION OF IDENTITY

The two girls exchanged a long look. Samantha couldn't help recalling how excited Mrs. Billingsley had been about the Blue Star—and how she had been determined to own it. "I have to show this envelope to Mademoiselle," said Nellie. "I'll take all these papers to her."

"I don't think the Admiral wants us to visit Mademoiselle," Samantha warned.

"I won't stay long," Nellie promised. She snatched up the papers. "I'll see you after dinner," she added as she hurried out of the cabin.

It was a lonely dinner for Samantha. Charlotta pointedly ignored her throughout the meal, while the Admiral and Grandmary again became involved in conversation with Captain Newman. Luckily, however, the Professor had brought Plato along, and Samantha enjoyed watching the little monkey scamper around the dining room in his white bow tie. When Plato jumped up on her shoulders and tried to pull out her hair ribbon, she picked him up gently and held him on her lap. The gold locket she wore fascinated the monkey, and he happily toyed with the shiny chain.

"Is he bothering you?" Harry asked after a few minutes. "If so, I'll take him away."

"He's not bothering me at all," said Samantha. "He's fun."

"Hah!" snorted Charlotta with a toss of her blond curls. "I'm not surprised that you enjoy the company of monkeys."

They're nicer than some people! Samantha wanted to say, but instead she just smiled at Plato and offered him a piece of green bean.

"I hope these last two days haven't been too hard for you," Harry said as Samantha played with the little monkey. "I'm sure you miss Mademoiselle Étienne."

"Yes, Nellie and I both do," said Samantha.

"It's a terrible business," Harry sympathized, and then lowering his voice, he confided to Samantha, "My uncle is so upset, he's hardly slept the last two nights. He's still hoping the

Blue Star will be found. But, well..." Harry's voice trailed off.

"You don't think Mademoiselle Étienne stole it, do you?" Samantha asked.

Harry said slowly, "I would *hate* to think of Mademoiselle Étienne as a thief. She seems such a pleasant young lady." He hesitated and then added, "But why did someone send her that note? And if she's innocent, why did she rip it up?"

"Maybe the note was meant for someone else," Samantha suggested.

"It had Mademoiselle's initials on it, didn't it?" Harry asked.

"Yes," Samantha agreed reluctantly. "That doesn't mean Mademoiselle is guilty, though." She looked down at Plato, who was still playing with her shiny locket, and decided to try out her earlier theory again. "Maybe Plato took the Blue Star—he likes bright, sparkly things—and then he threw it overboard. That would explain why it hasn't been found."

Harry nodded thoughtfully. "I think it's more than likely that the thief—whoever it was—got scared and threw the sapphire overboard. It could have been Plato. As I've explained to my uncle, we'll probably never know for sure."

We'll probably never know for sure. Harry's words, so much like Grandmary's, echoed in Samantha's mind through the rest of the dinner. *We have to find out the answer,* she told herself. *No matter what it is.*

After dinner, the Admiral and Captain Newman persuaded Professor Wharton to join them in the saloon for a game of cards. The Captain invited Harry to join them, too, but Professor Wharton interfered. "Harry's too experienced a cardplayer to play with a bunch of amateurs like us—aren't you, Harry?"

"You flatter me, Uncle," Harry said with a smile. "Tonight, however, I have work to do. I need to have your letters ready to send out tomorrow."

Before joining the cardplayers, the Admiral

escorted Samantha back to her cabin. As they walked down the narrow passageway, Samantha explained to him that Nellie needed to post an envelope to someone in Ireland.

"Not a bit of a problem," the Admiral assured her. "The crew will collect the passengers' outgoing mail early tomorrow morning, just before we get to Queenstown. They'll add it to the other mailbags the ship brought from New York. Tell Nellie to address her envelope and ask Doris to give it to me. I'll see that it goes out with the other passengers' mail."

Samantha was hesitant to ask for another favor, but she decided to try. "Do you think it might be possible for us to visit Queenstown—just while the ship is docked in the port?"

The Admiral looked puzzled by her question. "Only the mail boat is going into Queenstown, along with some steerage passengers, of course," he said. Then he smiled. "But we will visit London and Paris!"

"Yes, London and Paris will be wonderful," Samantha agreed, not wishing to seem ungrateful. They had reached Cabin 7. "Thank you," she added. "And thank you for posting Nellie's envelope."

Samantha slipped into the cabin. A light was on in the parlor, and she heard snoring coming from Doris's room. But as she looked into her and Nellie's room, she discovered it was empty.

As Samantha sat on the bottom berth, she realized that she should never have let Nellie visit Mademoiselle Étienne alone. What if the French tutor really was the thief? What if some harm had come to Nellie?

She listened for any sound from the hallway, hoping that Nellie would return. The ship was tossing in the waves, however, and Samantha could hear only the wind and rain outside. Soon, she decided that she had to look for Nellie. As quietly as she could, she let herself out of the cabin and went down the dark halls of the empty first-class section.

It took her a few minutes to find Cabin 32. It was at the end of a dimly lit corridor, the last in the row. Samantha was gathering her courage to knock on the door when she heard a woman's voice inside the room declare angrily, "You'll be sorry!"

There was a muttered reply, and then the sound of footsteps. Samantha barely had time to jump into the dark corner at the end of the hall before the cabin door was flung open. She pressed herself against the wall and hoped that the creaking of the ship would hide the sound of her breathing.

A woman rushed out of the cabin and stormed down the hallway. She was in too much of a hurry to notice Samantha hiding in the shadows. But Samantha saw her quite clearly. It was Mrs. Billingsley!

11
LOST AND FOUND

Her back pressed against the wood paneling, Samantha squeezed into the shadowy corner, terrified that Mrs. Billingsley would turn and see her. *What had Mrs. Billingsley been doing in Mademoiselle Étienne's cabin? And where was Nellie?*

Mrs. Billingsley's plump figure turned and disappeared down another corridor. Then the door to Cabin 32 opened a crack. Samantha pulled herself back into the shadows. She held her breath as the door opened wider.

A thin figure wrapped in a shawl stepped out of the door and started walking quickly down the hall. As loudly as she dared, Samantha whispered, "Nellie?"

Nellie jumped and then whirled around.

"Oh, I'm so glad it's you!" she whispered as Samantha ran up to her. "Let's get back to our cabin. I have lots to tell you."

The girls entered their cabin, being careful not to wake Doris. They slipped into their room and sat down together on the lower berth. Nellie hugged her warm shawl around her shoulders and explained that she had left the crumpled papers with Mademoiselle Étienne earlier in the evening. "About half an hour ago, I went to ask her if any of the handwriting on the papers reminded her of the writing on the note. She said that one person's did."

Nellie paused. "Whose was it?" Samantha demanded.

"Well, before Mademoiselle could tell me, there was a knock on the door," Nellie explained. "Quick as I could, I hid up in the top berth and Mademoiselle Étienne put a blanket over me. Then I heard Mrs. Billingsley come in. At first, she was very nice—asking how Mademoiselle was, and did she need anything."

"Then what?" Samantha asked breathlessly.

"Then she told Mademoiselle that she wanted the Blue Star and was willing to buy it from her. She offered her a lot of money!"

"Really?" gasped Samantha.

"I heard her myself," Nellie said. "When Mademoiselle Étienne said that she didn't have the sapphire, Mrs. Billingsley didn't believe her. She offered even more money, but Mademoiselle kept telling her that she hadn't taken the Blue Star and had no idea where it was. Mrs. Billingsley got very mad and said she'd make things hard for Mademoiselle. Finally, she left and I got out of my hiding place."

"Jiminy!" exclaimed Samantha, her mind whirling. "So, it wasn't Mrs. Billingsley who took the sapphire. Was it her handwriting on the note?"

"No," said Nellie, her eyes widening. "It was Harry's!"

"Harry?" Samantha echoed.

"Well, Mademoiselle said she couldn't be sure, because she'd only looked at the note for a moment, but that's what she thought," Nellie explained. "She said that the handwriting on the note had reminded her of her beau's— that's why she'd been so excited to get the envelope. And she said that Harry's writing is a lot like his."

The two girls looked at each other. "I talked with him at dinner tonight," Samantha said, and she told Nellie what Harry had said about the note.

"He said Mademoiselle's initials were on it?" Nellie repeated.

"Yes," said Samantha. "And they were. I remember, because at first I saw the 'N' and I thought it was for you, but then I saw the 'E' and realized it was for Mademoiselle Étienne."

"But when Mademoiselle told everyone about the note yesterday, she said that it was 'addressed' to her," Nellie recalled. "She didn't say her initials were on the envelope."

"Are you sure?"

"Yes," Nellie insisted. "How could Harry have known?"

"Mademoiselle might've said something to the Captain and Professor Wharton later," Samantha suggested. "Or maybe—"

"Maybe it was Harry who wrote the note," Nellie finished for her.

Samantha frowned. "In that case, he lied to me. He said he didn't want to think that Mademoiselle Étienne was the thief."

Nellie thought for a moment. "What if *Harry* is the thief? He might have heard about the robbery at the Larchmonts' and thought it would be easy to make people suspect Mademoiselle."

"But why would he steal the Blue Star in front of a whole table full of people?" Samantha shook her head. "It doesn't make sense. He'd be bound to have lots of other chances when no one else was around."

"If no one else was around, the Professor would know for sure that it was Harry who'd stolen it," Nellie pointed out. "This way, he'd be the last person suspected."

"Perhaps," Samantha said, but she wasn't

convinced. She was suddenly tired, and she began to get ready for bed. As she unpinned her hairbow and began to brush out her hair, she asked Nellie, "All the men were searched, even Harry and the Professor. Do you really think Harry could have hidden the sapphire somewhere in the dining room?"

Nellie shook her head. "I don't know. But I think we should search the room again tonight."

"Tonight?" Samantha protested. "We've already searched it, and so have the Professor and Jack. Nobody found anything, remember?"

"A few things were found," Nellie reminded her. She pulled out their notes on the suspects. On the back, in writing made uneven by the ship's rolling, Nellie jotted down a list:

> *a button*
> *a long piece of string*
> *pennies*
> *a wine cork*
> *a few sewing pins*
> *a bent nail*

"I don't know if it's worth going back to look again tonight," Samantha said doubtfully as she looked at the list. "It's awfully late and it's stormy outside. And what if Doris finds out that we've both left the cabin in the middle of the night?"

"We won't go on the outside decks at all," Nellie promised. "But we have to do *something* to help Mademoiselle Étienne. She isn't eating or sleeping. And she's terribly worried about her grandfather and what he'll think if she's accused of a crime."

Samantha listened to the wind howling outside and for a moment she hesitated. But at last she told Nellie, "You're right." She started pinning up her hair again. "We have to try to help."

It was well past midnight as the girls made their way down the deserted corridors to the Captain's dining room. The storm outside had grown worse, and the floor rose and fell as the ship tossed in the crashing waves.

When they reached the dining room, they

closed the door after themselves and then turned on the room's single electric lamp. By its dim light, they looked around the portholes, over the serving table, and around each chair. They found nothing except a few dust balls.

Nellie knelt down by the dining table. "Well," she said as she ran her hands along the table's underside. "Someone likes to chew gum." She lifted the tablecloths and pointed to a dried wad of gum stuck under the table. "Look, it's right where Harry was sitting when the sapphire was stolen. I wonder if he left it there."

"We'd get into trouble for doing that at school. But it's not exactly a crime," said Samantha. "Here, let me see."

As Samantha leaned under the table to examine the gum, one of the hairpins she had hastily stuck in her hair caught in the lace tablecloth. "Ow!" she cried as the tablecloth tangled and pulled on her hair. Nellie helped her to untangle the cloth. Then both girls stood up. As they smoothed the tablecloths back into place, Samantha thought of something. "The person who pulled the tablecloth didn't *have* to be sitting over there." She pointed to the opposite side of the table. "Someone sitting right here could have moved it from *underneath* the table."

Nellie looked at her as if she were crazy. "Don't you think people would have noticed if someone had been crawling under the table?"

"Yes, but remember what was found on the floor, underneath the table?" Samantha said excitedly. "Pins and that long piece of string. What if someone pinned the string to the edge of this cloth"—she held up the heavy linen tablecloth—"and then pulled the string from the *other* side of the table?"

Nellie thought for a long moment. "I don't think it would work," she told Samantha finally. "If you fastened a long string to the tablecloth, the string would just hang straight down. Someone on the other side of the table wouldn't be able to find it and pull it at just the right moment."

Samantha pointed to the gum underneath the table. "Not if you used chewing gum. You could stick the string to that, and then put it somewhere handy. Then all you'd have to do is reach under the table and pull."

"And that's just where Harry was sitting," said Nellie, beginning to catch Samantha's enthusiasm. "Do you really think he could have done it?"

Samantha nodded vigorously. "Yes! It would only take a minute to arrange the string. And remember, he was the first one at the table that night. He was sitting here alone when we came in."

"What if Harry—" Nellie began, but she stopped as the door suddenly opened. Harry walked in, with Plato dangling from his shoulders.

"Did someone mention my name?" Harry asked with a smile.

12
DANGER AT SEA

Harry closed the door and then leaned casually against it. "Plato and I were just passing by and we saw the light on. What are you girls doing?"

Samantha tried to answer, but her tongue felt thick and useless in her mouth. She shot a glance at Nellie and saw that she had gone white. Both girls started to back away from Harry.

"What's the matter? Cat got your tongues?" Harry asked. He walked farther into the room, with Plato chattering on his shoulder.

"N–no," stuttered Samantha, struggling to speak. "We were—we were just trying to remember where everyone was sitting the night the sapphire was stolen." Now that she was actually talking, the words tumbled out. Before she knew what she was doing, she had pointed to a chair. "You were sitting here, weren't you?"

Samantha was furious at herself for asking such a question. Harry didn't seem upset, though. "Why yes, I believe I was," he agreed. He stopped next to the table. He was smiling, but his eyes looked cold and calculating. "It's a bit late to be playing detective, isn't it?" he asked, casually resting his hands on the table.

"We were going to leave soon," Nellie said.

"Very soon," Samantha chimed in.

Harry leaned forward a bit, and Plato chose that moment to escape. He jumped from Harry's shoulders onto the table and then ran across the floor. Harry glanced at a porthole, and they could all hear the waves pounding outside. "The weather is getting worse by the minute," Harry said calmly. "Why don't you girls let Plato and me walk you to your cabin? We're going that way ourselves." He turned to the monkey. "Come, Plato!"

Plato ignored him, choosing to climb up to a porthole instead. Outside, the wind howled and the ship rolled and heaved in the waves. Samantha was suddenly very sure that she didn't want to go anywhere with Harry. She decided that she had to tell a white lie. "No, thank you," she said. "You and Plato can go ahead. The Admiral is going to meet us here. In fact, he should be here any moment. We'll just wait for him."

Harry smiled slightly. "I'm afraid you're mistaken," he told her. "The Admiral and my uncle are playing cards in the saloon. That reporter fellow is with them, too. They'll be busy for quite some time. I'll take you to them."

Samantha had a sudden vision of walking down the open passageway to the saloon—with the angry waves crashing into the ship and Harry walking just behind her. She remembered the Admiral's warning: *Passengers, especially children, have been known to fall overboard from slippery decks.*

"No! We'll just wait here," Samantha said

desperately. Out of the corner of her eye, she saw Plato heading toward the door, and a sudden hope occurred to her. Samantha looked over at Nellie, who seemed to catch her meaning.

"We're not in a hurry," Nellie told Harry firmly.

Looking over Harry's shoulder, Samantha eyed Plato. *If you are ever going to cause trouble, Plato, please do it now,* she begged silently.

Harry shook his head. "No, I insist," he said, and he began to walk around the table toward Samantha and Nellie. He had almost reached them when a bell began to clang. Plato was swinging on the bell rope that summoned the steward.

Cursing the monkey under his breath, Harry lunged for him, but Plato jumped nimbly out of the way. Harry was still chasing the monkey around the dining room when a sleepy-looking steward entered.

"Did someone call?" he asked.

"Yes!" Samantha spoke up before Harry

could answer. "Would you please get the Admiral from the saloon? Tell him Samantha and Nellie are in the dining room waiting for him."

The steward left, and a few minutes later, the Admiral entered the dining room, followed by Captain Newman, the Professor, and Jack.

"What are you girls doing here?" the Admiral demanded, anger and concern mixed in his voice. "You should have been in bed hours ago. It's much too dangerous for you to be walking around on a night like this."

"That's what I told them, sir," agreed Harry.

"We want to show you something," Nellie said, refusing to look at Harry.

"Any sign of the Blue Star?" the Professor asked eagerly.

"No," Samantha admitted. "But we have found some clues." Together, she and Nellie showed the Admiral and the others the chewing gum under the table, right by Harry's seat. Then they illustrated how, if the tablecloth had been pinned to a string, it could have been pulled from the opposite side of the table.

"The chewing gum would have kept the string in place," Nellie pointed out. "So whoever was sitting here"—she tapped on Harry's chair—"could have pulled the tablecloth and it would have looked as if someone across the table did it."

The Admiral listened carefully. "Interesting," he commented.

"Yes," agreed Captain Newman. "But it's hardly proof."

"The note!" Nellie whispered. Samantha nodded, and then she told the Captain how Mademoiselle Étienne had thought Harry's handwriting looked like the writing on the note she had received.

"She wasn't sure it was the same," Nellie added. "But she thought it was."

Jack gave a long whistle, and then he looked at Harry appraisingly.

"This is ridiculous," Harry said patiently. "Miss Étienne is suspected of a serious crime. It's not surprising that she would be eager to throw suspicion on someone else." He turned to Samantha and Nellie. "I know you girls want to believe that *anyone* other than your tutor could have taken the sapphire, but you're simply making up theories. Why, I don't even chew gum. That disgusting wad has probably been there for months, anyway."

Jack knelt down and examined the gum. He looked up at Harry. "I've chewed a lot of gum in my time, and this doesn't look all that old to me."

"Uncle," Harry appealed to the Professor. "You know I would never steal from you. And if I wanted to take the Blue Star, why do it at a table filled with people? I've had plenty of other opportunities. Besides, I was searched like all the other men. I couldn't possibly have taken the sapphire out of this room."

Jack stood up. His eyes were flashing, and he looked like a terrier eagerly following a scent. "How do we know the Blue Star was in this room to begin with? I didn't actually see the sapphire in the box that night. Did anyone else here?"

The room was silent. Samantha suddenly recalled that Nellie had said she'd never even seen the Blue Star. *I didn't see it that night either,* Samantha realized.

"It's occurred to me that maybe the box was already empty when the Professor went to open it," Jack continued. "That's why nobody found the Blue Star that night. It wasn't here."

"That's absurd!" declared the Professor. "I would have known that the box was empty as soon as I felt its weight."

"I'd considered that," allowed Jack. "But what if someone who knew exactly how heavy the sapphire felt had weighed the box down— say, with pennies?"

The Professor put one hand on the table to steady himself, but he said nothing. "Why didn't you mention this theory before?" the Admiral asked Jack.

"Because only the Professor or Harry would have had the opportunity to take the Blue Star before the box was opened at dinner," Jack explained. He glanced down at the table.

"Before tonight I didn't think either of them could have pulled down the tablecloth—they were sitting on the wrong side of the table. Now the girls have convinced me that Harry could have done it."

Everyone looked at Harry, and his handsome face turned bright red. "You're not going to believe the imaginings of a couple of schoolgirls, are you?" he asked his uncle.

Professor Wharton frowned. "Harry, I know that you had some scrapes with the law when you were young, yet I've always believed that I could trust you." He took a deep breath. "In the interest of fairness, however, I suppose we must explore every possibility."

Harry threw up his hands in disgust. "If you really think that I took your precious sapphire, search me again!" he declared angrily. "Search my room! Look through everything I own! I guarantee that you won't find it, because I don't have it!"

The Admiral coughed discreetly and nodded to Samantha and Nellie. "Girls," he said, "I think it's time for you to retire to your cabin."

Samantha and Nellie followed the Admiral out of the dining room. As they walked down the passageway to the first-class cabins, he lectured them sternly. "I know you had the best of intentions, but you mustn't play detective anymore. You might become involved in a very dangerous situation."

Samantha remembered the cruel look in Harry's eyes and how he had insisted on walking them to the saloon. *What might have happened?* she wondered with a shiver. But all she said was, "Yes, *Grand-père.*"

The Admiral softened. "*Grand-père,* eh?"

"I learned it from Mademoiselle Étienne," Samantha reminded him.

Nellie looked up at the Admiral shyly. "Mademoiselle really is very nice. It would be terrible if she were accused of a crime she didn't commit."

"Don't worry," the Admiral said as they reached Cabin 7. "We'll investigate your theory about young Harry, and his belongings will be thoroughly searched."

"Will you let us know if the Blue Star is found?" Samantha asked urgently as they stood in front of the door. "Even if we're asleep, will you wake us up?"

"You will be informed immediately," the Admiral promised. "No matter what time it is." He turned to go, then stopped. "And, Nellie, don't forget to give your envelope to Doris. The mail goes out in the morning."

"Thank you," Nellie said. "I'll remember."

Samantha and Nellie were careful not to wake Doris as they got ready for bed. Nellie sealed Jamie's money in an envelope, addressed it, and left it on the table, with a note for Doris to give the envelope to the Admiral. Then the two girls hurried to their room.

"I'm sure we're right about Harry," Nellie whispered when she was in her berth.

"I'm sure, too," Samantha whispered back from the upper bunk. "But do you think they'll find the Blue Star?"

"They've got to find it," Nellie said confidently.

As the storm raged outside their cabin, Samantha tried to stay awake, expecting to hear the Admiral's knock on their cabin door at any moment. Finally, however, sleep overcame her.

She woke to find that the storm had ended and the sun was shining brightly through the porthole. Samantha's heart started racing. She remembered the Admiral's promise to wake her when the sapphire was found—yet she had slept through the night.

"Nellie!" she called out anxiously. "Did anyone knock on the door last night?"

She heard Nellie rustling in the blankets below. "No," Nellie replied sleepily. Then her voice sounded wide-awake. "Oh, Samantha, they must not have found the Blue Star!"

Samantha felt her stomach twist, like a handkerchief being wrung out to dry. *Were we wrong about everything?*

13

AN UNEXPECTED PACKAGE

Samantha and Nellie were dressed within minutes. In the cabin's little parlor, Doris was busy sewing. "I gave the Admiral your envelope," she told the girls. "But don't disturb him this morning. He's awful tired. He said he was up late."

"Did he find anything last night?" Samantha asked.

"Eh?" Doris inquired, putting her hand to her ear.

"DID HE FIND ANYTHING?"

Doris looked confused. "Not as I know of."

Samantha and Nellie looked at each other. "Let's go up to the saloon," Samantha suggested. "Maybe someone up there has heard something."

An Unexpected Package

They put on their coats and walked upstairs to the promenade deck. When they were halfway down the open-air passageway, Harry came out of the saloon. He saw Samantha and Nellie walking toward him and stopped. "Well, if it isn't the girl detectives!"

He stood in the middle of the passageway so that the girls couldn't get past him. "Do you know that all my things were searched last night and nothing, absolutely nothing, was found?" he demanded. "What do you say to that?"

Samantha saw the mean look of triumph on Harry's face, and she felt almost sick with despair. She couldn't think of anything to say. But Nellie stepped up to Harry. "Excuse us," she said loudly. "We need to get through." She took Samantha's arm, and together they pushed past him.

"Next time, you'd better think before you accuse someone," Harry shouted after them.

As soon as she and Nellie were inside the warm saloon, Samantha took a deep breath.

"You were very brave out there," she said to Nellie.

Nellie shrugged. "He's just a bully," she said scornfully. "And I'm sure he stole the sapphire. I wish we could prove it!"

Samantha nodded sadly. Together they stood by the wide windows and looked out at the sea. It was a clear, bright morning, and the sun glistened off the waves. In the distance, they could dimly see Ireland's coast. For several long minutes, the girls stared at the sea in silence. "Well, at least something has gone right," Samantha said finally. "Jamie's package will go out with the mail this morning."

"Yes," Nellie agreed halfheartedly. "I suppose that's something."

"The mail boat should arrive soon," Samantha continued. Then she clapped a hand over her mouth. "Jiminy!"

Nellie turned to her in surprise. "What is it?"

Samantha grabbed her friend's hand. "The mail boat! Come on! We have to find the Admiral!"

An Unexpected Package

Together, Samantha and Nellie ran out of the saloon, down the steps, and toward the first-class cabins. When they reached Cabin 8, Samantha pounded on the door. Finally, she heard the Admiral's voice saying, "Just a moment!"

When the Admiral opened the door, he was wearing his dressing gown and rubbing his eyes. "What is it, girls?"

"Did anyone check the mail?" Samantha asked breathlessly.

"What?"

"The mail!" she repeated. "Harry was writing lots of letters, and I'll bet he put them out in the mailbag. Maybe he put the Blue Star in the mailbag, too."

Suddenly the Admiral looked wide-awake. "It just might be possible," he said, almost to himself. "Wait here," he told Samantha and Nellie. "I'll be with you in a moment."

The Admiral hurriedly dressed, and then he, Samantha, and Nellie went to call on Captain Newman in his dayroom. The two men spoke privately for a few minutes. Whatever the Admiral said must have convinced Captain Newman, because he ordered one of the stewards to bring him the passengers' outgoing mail.

When Samantha first saw the canvas mailbag marked "R.M.S. *Queen Caroline*," her heart sank. It was too small to contain many packages. *What if we're wrong again!* she worried.

The burly steward opened up the bag. It was almost entirely full of envelopes. A few of the envelopes were large, but none of them looked big enough to hold the Blue Star. There was, however, one heavy, square package labeled "Books." According to the addresses written on the front, it was being sent from Professor Wharton to Harrison J. Wharton III.

Captain Newman chewed thoughtfully on his pipe when he saw the package. "Ask Professor Wharton and his nephew to join us in here," he told the steward.

An Unexpected Package

The Professor arrived first, with Plato, who looked half-asleep, resting on his shoulder. The circles under the Professor's eyes were darker than ever, and his face was unshaven. He told the Captain that he didn't recognize the package and had no idea what books might be in it. "I suppose," he said doubtfully, "that Harry might be sending some of our research books back home. I always leave these details to him."

Just then Harry stepped into the office. "What's this all about?" he asked angrily. "I was trying to sleep when—" Harry broke off his complaint when he saw the package on Captain Newman's desk. "Why is that here?"

Captain Newman eyed him carefully. "Would you open it, please?" he asked in an even tone.

Harry crossed his arms defiantly. "No, I'd rather not. I'm tired of this ridiculous persecution. And you have no right to open a private package!"

An awkward silence filled the cabin.

Samantha and Nellie looked at each other anxiously. *Something important must be in the package!* Samantha thought. *But what if Harry won't allow us to open it?*

The Professor cleared his throat. "Since the package is supposedly from me, I presume that I have the right to open it."

"This is ridiculous," Harry sputtered as his uncle began to unwrap the brown paper surrounding the package. "I refuse to be a part of it." He turned to leave.

"Not yet," said Captain Newman, and the steward blocked the door.

There were three books in the package. The Professor glanced at the first two books and said they were standard texts on archaeology. Then the Professor picked up the third book. "I've never seen this one before." He began to thumb through the pages, but halfway through he stopped, his brows furrowed. He laid the open book on the Captain's desk, and Samantha could see that the pages had been hollowed out.

An Unexpected Package

Resting inside the hollow was a velvet pouch.

The Professor took a deep breath. Then he reached into the pouch and pulled out the Blue Star. The morning sun was streaming through the porthole as the Professor held the sapphire up to the light. The radiant blue stone sparkled like a star in ice.

Samantha felt someone squeeze her hand. "We found it!" Nellie whispered.

The Professor gazed at the Blue Star for a moment. Then he turned to his nephew in disbelief. "How could you have done such a thing?"

"It's your fault!" Harry exploded at his uncle. "We could've gotten a fortune for the Blue Star, but you wouldn't sell it. You don't care that I need money. You care more about archaeology than you do your own family!"

Harry's angry words startled Plato. Looking anxious, the little monkey clung to the Professor's jacket and chattered nervously. "It's all right, Plato," the Professor soothed him. Then he turned to his nephew. "I could have forgiven you for betraying me, Harry," he said sadly. "But you tried to place the blame for your crime on an innocent girl. That I can't forgive."

"Nothing would have happened to her," Harry protested. "There wasn't any proof against her."

The Professor quietly put the Blue Star back into the velvet pouch. Then he turned to Captain Newman. "I am sorry for all the trouble we have caused you. Would you please keep my nephew safely locked up until we get to London? By then, I should have decided what to do with him."

"At least I won't have to put up with your blasted monkey anymore!" Harry yelled over his shoulder as the steward escorted him away.

While the Professor stayed to talk with Captain Newman, the Admiral ushered Samantha and Nellie out of the office. As they reached the main deck, they could see the coast of Ireland growing larger on the horizon.

An Unexpected Package

They were close enough now to see the outline of buildings on the distant shore.

"Girls," the Admiral announced as they neared the first-class cabins, "I am going to go and offer my profound apologies to Mademoiselle Étienne. I will also tell her how you two young ladies proved her innocence."

"It was Nellie, really," Samantha said. "She knew Mademoiselle Étienne wouldn't have done such a thing. She believed in Mademoiselle."

Nellie turned to her. "But you believed in me, Samantha—even when I wouldn't speak to you, you still trusted me."

"Well," said the Admiral with mock sternness, "*I* believe both of you girls deserve a reward. Dress warmly and meet me on deck in an hour. That's when the mail boat is leaving for Queenstown. We're going to take a trip."

Nellie caught her breath, and Samantha almost jumped with excitement. "Are we really going to—"

"To visit Ireland? Yes, why not!" exclaimed the Admiral. "It's a beautiful country. Both of you girls should see it, but most of all you, Nellie, because it's your family's homeland."

Nellie looked up at him, her eyes shining. "I would like that more than anything," she said quietly. "Thank you..." She hesitated, and then added in almost a whisper, *"Grand-père."*

Within the hour, Samantha and Nellie were dressed in their warmest clothes and waiting on deck. The Admiral and Grandmary came up the stairs to join them.

Samantha was surprised to see her grandmother, but Grandmary just smiled. "I find that the fresh air does me good," she said. "Besides, travel is always enlightening. I decided that I really should see Ireland while I have the opportunity."

Grandmary, the Admiral, Samantha, and Nellie joined a few dozen returning immigrants on the mail boat. Mademoiselle Étienne came up on deck to wave good-bye to them, and Samantha was happy to see the tutor talking and laughing with Jack.

After the last bag of mail was loaded, the boat began steaming its way into Queenstown harbor. The wind was freezing and a faint mist of rain was falling, but Nellie glowed with joy. "Oh, Samantha!" she exclaimed. "I can't believe how lucky we are to be here."

Samantha grinned and pushed back a strand of wet hair that had straggled over her eyes. "I can't believe it either," she agreed. "And the best part of it is, our adventures are just beginning!"

WHITE STAR LINE.
"OLYMPIC."
45,000 TONS.
AND
"TITANIC."
45,000 TONS.
THE LARGEST STEAMER
IN THE WORLD.

LOOKING BACK

A PEEK INTO THE PAST

An ocean liner gets a festive send-off.

In Samantha's time, faster forms of travel and communication made it easier than ever before to learn about and visit other countries. As the world grew smaller, Americans developed an intense interest in other lands and cultures.

Europe was an especially popular destination for people who could afford to travel. Like Grandmary and the Admiral, well-to-do Americans wanted to see Europe's great cities, such as London, Paris, and Rome. There they could enjoy fine hotels and food and, at the same time, become more "cultured" by visiting world-famous theaters, opera houses, symphony halls, museums, and castles.

Crossing the ocean could be a grand experience in itself. Just a few decades earlier, ocean travel had been slow, dangerous, and very uncomfortable. But improved steamships in the 1870s made the voyage safer and faster. By the time Samantha was a girl, so many Americans were traveling abroad that shipping companies competed wildly to build the biggest, fastest, and most luxurious ocean liners.

Postcards from London and Paris

Although the *Queen Caroline,* the ship Samantha takes in the story, was modest and a bit old-fashioned, some ocean liners in the early 1900s were practically floating palaces. They featured vast ballrooms with vaulted ceilings and marble floors, tropical garden rooms decked out with palm trees and live birds, and velvet-draped dining rooms where lavish

175

An elegant parlor for first-class passengers—notice the stained-glass ceiling!

meals were served. The cabins, too, could be unbelievably luxurious—some were even decorated to look like rooms in Egyptian palaces or French castles!

The finery was for first-class passengers only, though. Second-class passengers stayed in simpler accommodations on a lower deck. Even deeper in the ship was steerage, where passengers paying only $10 or $15 for the week-long voyage stayed in dim, cramped quarters and had little more than bread and soup to eat.

On crossings from Europe, steerage would be crammed with people emigrating to America. Crossings to Europe, however, had few steerage passengers—mostly immigrants who had given up on America and were returning home, like those who left Samantha's ship at Queenstown.

Because of the large number of immigrants leaving Ireland in the early 1900s, Queenstown was a busy port and many steamships stopped there. But in Samantha's day, unlike today, Ireland was not a popular tourist destination. Many Americans were prejudiced against Irish immigrants and did not consider their homeland a fashionable place to visit.

Queenstown (now called Cobh) as it looks today

177

Americans were fascinated, however, by far-away places that seemed exotic and mysterious. Readers devoured books describing

Tourists in Egypt

travelers' experiences in little-known parts of the world. Wealthy Americans with a taste for adventure traveled to remote destinations such as Japan, China, or Egypt.

People were captivated by the romance and adventure of past civilizations, too. Archaeologists were unearthing the remains of ancient civilizations around the world. Museums in America and Europe put on dazzling displays of archaeological discoveries and other precious objects, such as exceptionally rare or large jewels. Newspaper reports of these spectacular finds created tremendous excitement, and some

Popular magazines featured articles on exotic places and people.

archaeologists, like the fictional Professor Wharton, became celebrities. Stories abounded of curses associated with the artifacts they found—much like the tales of bad luck that surrounded the fictional Blue Star.

Archaeologist Arthur Evans gained fame in 1903 for discovering an ancient civilization on the Greek island of Crete.

In Samantha's time, people could view the world's largest and most famous sapphire right in New York City. In 1900, the American Museum of Natural History acquired the legendary Star of India, a deep-blue sapphire nearly the size of a small hen's egg. It had been discovered in the Asian country of Sri Lanka two centuries earlier. You can see the Star of India—along with many of the world's most fabulous gems and minerals—in the same museum today.

The Star of India sapphire— at about its actual size!

GLOSSARY OF FRENCH WORDS

NOTE: *In the pronunciation guides below, the letters "zh" are pronounced like the "s" in the word "treasure."*

au revoir (*oh ruh-vwar*)—good-bye

bonsoir (*bohn-swahr*)—good evening

bonjour (*bohn-zhoor*)—hello, good morning

fleur (*fler*)—flower

grand-père (*grahn-pehr*)—grandfather

ma chérie (*mah sheh-ree*)—my dear

madame (*mah-dahm*)—Mrs., ma'am

mademoiselle (*mahd-mwa-zehl*)—Miss

mal de mer (*mahl duh mehr*)—seasickness

maman (*mah-mahn*)—mama

monsieur (*muh-syer*)—Mr., sir

n'est-ce pas? (*ness pah*)—Isn't that right? Isn't it so?

Nicole Étienne (*nee-kohl eh-tyen*)

oui (*wee*)—yes

voilà (*vwah-lah*)—There it is.

ABOUT THE AUTHOR

Sarah Masters Buckey grew up in New Jersey, where her favorite hobbies were swimming in the summer, sledding in the winter, and reading all year round.

She and her family now live in New Hampshire. She is the author of *The Curse of Ravenscourt: A Samantha Mystery* and *Samantha's Special Talent*. She also wrote three American Girl History Mysteries: *The Smuggler's Treasure, Enemy in the Fort*, and *Gangsters at the Grand Atlantic*, which was nominated for the 2004 Agatha Award for Best Children's/Young Adult Mystery.